Nightmare Yearnings

Stories by
Eric Raglin

Cover Art/Design: Matthew Revert

Editor: Rachel Oestreich, Owner/Editor of The Wallflower Editing, LLC

Interior Design, Typesetting, and Layout: Sam Richard

CONTENTS

MOTHER'S TONGUE

Mom claims I changed after drowning at Adventureland. I was a girl of six, unaccompanied but wearing inflatable water wings. You might think my mom was wrong to let me swim alone, especially in the wave pool, but you're misunderstanding her parenting philosophy. She named me River, if that tells you anything. Yep, River drowned. Hardee har har. I've heard it before.

There I was in the water, waiting for the next wave to come in. The water wings were biting into my armpits, so I wriggled out of them. Just as they came loose, the wave hit me full force, knocking me into a group of screaming teenagers and whisking the water wings out of reach. I immediately went under, thrashing my arms to stay afloat like I'd seen other kids do, but to no effect. The teens did nothing as I sank. With my eyes glassy and stinging, I watched as, half-submerged, they bounced around and fondled each other. Air bubbles trickled out of my lungs, slowly at first and then in larger bursts, looking like clear clusters of grapes climbing to the surface. My lungs felt hot, like a sunburn, and the burning became unbearable. I kicked my legs and went nowhere. A shadow came over the teens, over everything, eclipsing my vision. But in that darkness, a new light seeped in, enveloping me and easing the pain in my lungs, melting away my desire for air.

There was a song, undistorted in the water but still distant, as if sung from the opposite side of an empty football stadium. It was hard to identify its source, but when my throat began seizing, I noticed the tongues. Seven of them, long and pale, sticking out of the pool drain, vibrating in harmony. I couldn't make out the meaning. If it was words, it was a language I didn't yet understand, a language I could learn if I stayed under just a minute longer, though it was beyond my human abilities.

I don't remember much after that, only that I washed ashore like a castaway. When I awoke, a lifeguard was doing chest compressions and Mom was crowding the space, slapping my face gently at first and then not so gently. The lifeguard tried to shoo her away, but she wouldn't budge. It was only when I coughed up a cup of chlorine that they stopped arguing. The lifeguard backed off while Mom clutched me and wept.

She didn't know the lifeguard had broken my ribs, so she squeezed me tight. It hurt, but I didn't react. Overwhelmed, she squeezed tighter, kissing me and whispering promises in my ear. A rib shifted farther out of place, crunching hollow in my chest. I didn't scream or cry. What was a little pain? What use was my body, anyway?

———

CYNTHIA BEGS me not to do it. She also begged when I went spelunking, skydiving, and BASE jumping, but this time there are actual tears in her eyes.

"The park is cool enough on its own," she says, pulling up

a blog post titled "Best Things to Do at Yosemite" and thrusting it in my face. "You don't have to—"

"Babe, I'm driving," I say, batting the phone away.

The road is dirt, barely a single lane twisting and turning through the woods. Deer skirt the shoulder and I don't want to hit one.

"Oh," Cynthia says, "so you'll climb a mile-and-a-half-high rock wall without any gear, but using a phone while driving is too dangerous for you?"

"Goddamn, you're not gonna change my mind," I say. I slow the car down, not quite slamming the brakes.

Of course, she doesn't know why I have to do it—not the real reason. She figures I'm just an adrenaline junkie who can still be rehabilitated. I haven't told her about the tongues. I've never witnessed them as clearly as I did the day I drowned, but while jumping out of a plane or squeezing through a crawl space in an abandoned mine, I sometimes catch a glimpse—a white shape out of the corner of my eye, and if I'm lucky, the faintest hint of its song. The tighter I ride the line between life and death, the more I see and hear.

Cynthia wipes away her tears, smearing her eyeliner, then looks out the side window. I sigh and ease off the brakes, speeding up. It'll be another hour before we reach our campsite.

"Look," I say, "I know this is stressful for you, but—"

"Isn't it stressful for you too? Aren't you the least bit concerned you'll—"

She tries to say it but can't. My heart keeps a slow and steady beat, and my palms remain dry around the steering wheel. The best I can muster is a shrug in Cynthia's direction. She inhales sharply, closes her eyes, and begins muttering a prayer for me. If anyone else did this I'd assume they were being passive aggressive, but Cynthia is devout in her churchgoing and still says grace before each meal. As for me, I sleep in on Sunday mornings and like to eat my food while it's still hot.

After Cynthia's prayer, she's silent the rest of the ride. I try to pull her out of it when a coyote up ahead darts into the grass to snap at something, but her eyes don't follow where I'm pointing. I change tactics and, grinning, tune the radio to a country station. But even with Toby Keith's static-bathed voice blaring through the speaker, Cynthia keeps her head pressed against the glass, gazing into nothing. She doesn't even try to turn the music off. It's much less fun when I have to do it myself.

———

CYNTHIA BREAKS her silence while we're setting up our tent—or rather, while *I'm* setting it up. One of the pole clips keeps slipping, and after a few choice words, I call to her for help.

"Hey, Cyn, c'mon," I say, sweat in my eyes.

"If you can't set up a tent yourself, how are you gonna climb El Capitan?" she asks, rummaging through something in the car trunk.

She turns around with a bulging duffle bag slung over her shoulder. I figure her clothes are inside, but when she unzips it, it's full of brand-new climbing equipment—ropes, a harness, carabiners, the works. None of it is mine, but I know roughly how much it all costs, and it's certainly more than Cynthia can afford waitressing at Olive Garden.

"Why?" I ask, dropping the pole, the gray tent collapsing. "Just . . . why?"

"A compromise," she says. "You use all this in your climb and I won't break up with you."

"Jesus, you wasted so much money."

"What, to keep my girlfriend alive?"

I shake my head and, walking away from the tent, get to work on bear-proofing our food supplies. I find a tree branch that can hold everything and toss a rope over it.

"So, that's a no?" Cynthia says, following so close behind me I can feel her breath on my neck. I almost swat her away like a mosquito.

"Yes!" I say, and her face briefly lights up with a smile. "As in yes, that's a no."

She bites her lip, then throws the duffel bag at me. I catch it just barely, and by the time I set it down she's already halfway to the car.

"What," I shout, "are you going to drive off without me?"

"I wouldn't do that to you even if you are an idiot," she says, not looking back. "Keep the tent to yourself. I'll sleep in the car."

It's still an hour before dark, but she slams the door behind her and whips out a book, alternating between reading and staring off into space every few seconds. As soon as the sun dips below the canopy, she reclines her seat into something resembling a bed and doesn't come back out of the car.

I sleep alone in the tent, or try to anyway. Mostly I shift from one dirt clump to the next, occasionally finding a sharp rock in the middle of my spine. My sleeping bag does little to pad the ground, and the tent crinkles loudly each time I shift. When dawn finally comes, I've squeezed in barely an hour of rest. But in my few seconds of dreaming, I hear that song again, louder than I've heard it since Adventureland, alien melodies blending with real-world sounds—rain pattering against the tent flap, crickets chirping from some crevice beneath.

I wake to the smell of bacon and eggs. It's misty out, but Cynthia has a fire going—I'm not sure how, with all the rain

—and is hard at work seasoning an omelet. I rub the crust out of my eyes and try not to look exhausted.

"Morning," I say.

"Figured I'd make you one last breakfast before you fall to your death," Cynthia says, flipping the eggs on the pan. "How many slices of bacon do you want?"

"I'm giving up pork. Bad for the heart."

She frowns at me, then snorts and brings a fist to her mouth to hide her laugh. I can't help but crack a sleepy smile.

"Come eat with me," she says, slapping the wet stump beside her.

I pull up next to her, hoping she won't expect any more jokes out of me. My head feels foggy, and that pork joke is all my brain can muster until I've woken up a bit more. Cynthia scoops me up an omelet and grease quickly soaks through the paper plate. At this point the meal is more likely to put me in a food coma than give me energy, but I eat it anyway.

"You know why I'm doing this, right?" I ask between bites.

"Because you have a death wish and want to break my heart," Cynthia says.

"Well that, too, but . . ."

She doesn't laugh at that one, just sets her plate down in the dirt, looks me in the eyes, and waits. The morning mist sends a shiver through me, and I shovel down the rest of the omelet so I have an excuse not to talk. There's no point in completing the thought, anyway. No lie will satisfy Cynthia, and the truth will only land me in a mental institution.

———

I DRIVE extra slow on our way to El Capitan, hoping the night's rain will evaporate off the rock face before we arrive.

But as we pull up to it, the rock looks a shade darker than usual. I'll do some extra stretches before the ascent, give the sun some time to rise a bit more. I can't wait too long, though—if the rock gets too much sunlight, it'll be too hot to touch.

Cynthia unloads the duffle bag full of climbing gear, placing each item in front of me. When she takes out the harness, she kneels down as if to slip it over my legs, but I move away.

"I already told you no," I say.

And with that, Cynthia retreats back to the car and locks herself inside. She whips out her cell phone, dials a number, and steals a quick glance in my direction. When I finish my hamstring stretch, I amble over and knock on the glass. Whoever's on the other line is speaking, but I can't hear their words.

"Yes," Cynthia says, her voice muffled and shaky. "My girlfriend is trying to commit suicide. She's—yes, El Capitan. She—"

I pound on the glass, but Cynthia leans in the opposite direction and cups her free hand over the microphone.

"Don't listen to her, she's lying!" I shout through the glass, but Cynthia is already hanging up the call.

"They're coming," she says, and she shrugs, tossing her hands up in the air.

"Jesus fucking Christ."

The rock face is still dark with moisture, but Cynthia leaves me with no choice other than to proceed. If I don't do it now, it'll be years before we have the money to make another trip out here from Iowa. I stomp toward the rock wall, flexing and releasing my fists. My heart races, but I can't help it—I still yawn.

Then comes the song, carried on a gust of wind from atop the cliff. I crane my neck upward to get a glimpse but catch only the watery movement of what looks like a tongue slipping out of view. I thought it had just been a dream, but had the tongues actually come to me in the night? The song vibrates through me, my muscles twitching to life, adrenaline replacing ache. Now is the time.

———

THE THING about adrenaline is that it doesn't stay in your system long—an hour at most. Even with the song getting louder the farther I ascend, my arms start stiffening, becoming like rocks themselves. Whenever my other limbs feel secure, I take one hand off the rock wall to shake it, like a student three hours into a pen-and-paper test. I don't have a watch, but judging by the vast plain of rock above me, I'm only a fourth of the way there—still hours left. The wall is mostly dry by now, but some handholds are shadowed enough that their moisture hasn't simmered away. There are generally drier handholds to grab instead—ones that require me to stretch, sending fire through my calves. But sometimes those are too far away, and the slick handhold is my only option. In those moments, I hope Cynthia's prayers cling to me like armor.

Cynthia. I refuse to look down, but I know she's still there. Maybe sobbing in the car, gawking at the rock wall, gnawing her nails into oblivion. Most certainly she's waiting for emergency services to arrive and prevent me from "killing myself."

"Hi."

The voice is right next to me. I nearly let go of the wall but grip a jagged handhold just in time, the nail on my index finger bending backward and detaching. I grimace but focus on breathing and steadying myself. I close my eyes for a moment, but the thought that the climber beside me might just as suddenly close the distance and appear an inch from my face makes me open my eyes again.

She looks about my age. Like me, she doesn't have any gear, but her tank top and shorts have an '80s pink-and-blue color palette. How had I not seen someone so brightly dressed? I could have sworn I was the only climber undeterred by last night's rain.

"How—?" I start, but a rumble of thunder rolls through the sky, vibrating the stone beneath my hands and feet.

"Shoot," the woman says, smiling. "Better get climbing."

As she speaks, I think I see the nub of a second tongue, drained of pink and twisting, but she closes her mouth and resumes climbing before I can confirm it. She ascends with incredible haste and minimal thought, doesn't check that each handhold is secure, and—in a movement that makes my gut drop—actually leaps from one handhold to the next, momentarily leaving all four limbs free-floating. I'm about to yell at her when her body flickers. That's the best way I can describe it, like a TV losing power for half a second but not all the way. I blink to make sure nothing's in my eyes, but they're clear. The woman is making great time, and at this point I have to squint to see her; she's climbing more like she's a video game hero than a human.

Thunder again—louder, closer. The first sprinkle of rain lands in my eye—just a tiny drop, but it's enough. I'm done, and my training is for naught. I'll be back in flat-ass Iowa before I know it, farther from solving this mystery than ever before. I want to slam my fist against the rock, scream at the top of my lungs, but that isn't an option up here. I have to go back down.

Just as that thought pops into my head, the song grows louder, as if the storm has amplified it. Harmonic trills uncork chemicals in my brain and flood my system with emotions stronger than I've ever felt, even as a child. I weep. I cackle. I climb. Faster now, rain be damned.

"I'm coming, Mother!" the woman above me shouts, once more taking an apelike leap upward, shimmering out of existence for a nanosecond and then landing in place as solid as ever.

The flash of a tongue teases the edge of the cliff, and looking up at it, the woman whoops like a wolf. So she hears the song too; this "Mother" is not just last night's dream or a childhood hallucination.

The other climber is far ahead of me, but I'm keeping pace with her now, an alien strength possessing my muscles. Even in those moments, when one hand makes it and the other slips, I grit my teeth and pull myself up one-armed, daring the stone to deny me.

It's in this state that I fail to notice the helicopter. It's right beside me by the time I see it. Blades chopping, deafeningly loud even compared to the thunder. The rescuer calls to me, his voice faint.

"Ma'am, someone's coming down with a ladder," he says, his voice crackling through the speaker and made fuzzier by the electric air. "Stay where you are. He'll attach a harness to—"

I don't bother listening, I just climb. At this rate, I'll be there in half the time I originally projected, and depending on how bad the storm gets, the rescue pilot might deem it too dangerous to keep hovering beside me like the world's loudest horsefly.

"Ma'am, please," he says again, and I tune the rest out.

I know they won't try to grab me—too risky. But they'll yabber my ear off—beg me to consider all that life has to offer—until I get to the top. And sure, then I'll let them give me a ride down. But not until I see Mother—and more than just her harmonic tongues.

As soon as She crosses my mind, Her song changes key. No, "key" is too human a word for it—too of this world. The shift stirs something inside my chest, my heart pumping triple-time, delivering oxygen to my muscles so efficiently that I no longer feel any burn.

I'm like the other climber now, rocketing upward with one powerful bound after another. Each time I reconnect with the wall it scrapes my hands and bangs my knees, but I barely notice.

The other climber is even closer to the top. A single wing —part of Mother I've never seen—waves liquid-like over the ledge to beckon her. The climber finally grips the flat top— and yes, I'm sure of it now. Her body is static, fuzzy around the edges, like a channel losing signal. She peeks over the edge.

And that's when she screams, a sound so ripping it cuts through the thunder and the helicopter both. Her body drops, limbs seemingly boneless, falling and hurtling toward me. I leap out of the way and grip another handhold, but while still suspended, catch sight of the nub in her mouth. It's no longer a nub, though. It's a full tongue, long and pale and lapping upward in the gust of her descent. I swear I hear it vibrate, a high, buzzing pitch that bends lower the farther she drops—like a honking semi speeding by on the interstate. This is the beginning of Mother's tongue, the language behind the veil of death. The climber—a cosmic infant. Me— the unborn about to crown.

I'm ascending. There's no time to look down and see what happened to the woman, but I don't hear her land. My human tongue roves through my mouth, searching for a nub. The first nub of many, I hope. Up above, Mother's swimming wing floats on air, backlit and glistening as lightning splits the sky. I don't hear the thunder—Her song obliterates it.

And here her wing lowers, like a hand inviting me to

grasp it. All strength leaves me, and I realize I won't make it the ten feet to the top without Her help. Grant me mercy, Mother, please. Please.

I reach out.

———

CYNTHIA'S GONE. She followed EMS to the hospital but dips as soon as I wake up. When I try calling out to her, my words come out garbled. There are stitches inside my mouth and a gauze pad soaked with iron-tasting blood. As soon as I notice it, Cynthia vanishes—out of the intensive care wing and out of my mind.

A nurse walks in to change my IV.

"Uh mrrerr," I say, pantomiming putting on my face with a makeup mirror.

She nods, leaves the room, and comes back with her purse, the mirror inside. I grab it as soon as she holds it out to me, and it seems to weigh a ton in my hand. This must be how it feels the day after climbing El Capitan. Has it just been a day? I have no idea how long I was out. All I know is that I made it to the top. Everything after that is blank.

The mirror is dusted with old foundation. I point it at my face. With some effort, I open my mouth wide, and the nurse holds her hands out as if to stop me. My stitches strain. In the reflection is a gaping wound. No nub. No long, pale tongue. My human tongue is still there, but what does it matter? I glance over at the nurse, and she lowers her eyes.

"Whu happuh?" I ask, tears welling up.

The nurse hesitates, then sits down in the chair beside me. She grabs the mirror and places her hand over mine.

"You're very lucky," she says. "The doctor's never seen a tumor quite like it, and she had to operate immediately."

I turn away from her. The nurse sighs, pats my hand, and stands up.

"You could have died," she says, then walks out of the room.

But just as she says it, I feel something. A worm wriggling in the floor of my mouth—writhing and autonomous with a life of its own. I don't have the mirror anymore, but I slip a finger between my teeth. Something rises to touch it from the other side, warm and tingling.

I smile—Mother is still with me.

IVORY

"There's a place where the stars form a perfect ring, Lessi," Mom said. "And inside, there is no darkness." Her lips barely moved as she spoke, and her bone-thin limbs lay perfectly still. It was as if some parts of her had died before the others. Her eyes still glimmered with life, locked on to some point far beyond the white popcorn ceiling of her bedroom. Beyond what even the most powerful tele-scope could find. Tears trickled through the thin brown canyons of her wrinkles, and she smiled, exposing gums receded to thin pink crescents. But a smile was a smile. I squeezed her hand as if doing so might keep her soul from escaping. It didn't work.

———

IN THE MONTHS that followed Mom's death, I only left the house to check the mail. My work, online technical writing, didn't require me to go to an office, just someplace with a stable internet connection (i.e., my bed). As for running errands, there were apps for that. Someone brought me my groceries, my toiletries, even my antidepressants. Of course, I always requested they leave them at the door and to not bother knocking. I didn't want anyone—not even a stranger who'd forget my face five minutes later—to see me in this state: sour, greasy hair; pajama pants worn for two weeks straight without a wash; nose a perpetually sniffling mess. Some delivery drivers still knocked despite my instructions, and I froze up whenever it happened, as if making the slightest sound might have them kicking down the door.

Naturally, friends and family members reached out, sometimes with a call, sometimes a text. The calls I ducked on principle, but the texts—"How are things, Lessi? Been worried about you"—I responded to with a simple "fine, thx." These concerned messages eventually slowed to a trickle, which relieved me. I knew I should want people to check in with me, but there was something pleasant about spending every non-working, non-sleeping moment in front of the TV riding Mom's squeaky exercise bike. Well, okay, maybe "pleasant" is the wrong word. "Easy" is more like it. When I binged a season of *The Walking Dead* in a day, it required no thought, no reflection on the realities of my world. Neither did pedaling away on the exercise bike. It was a meditation in two simple words: "left, right, left, right . . ."

Four months into my grief, during my weekly trip to the mailbox, I found a letter from my aunt Mila. She still lived in Toluca and, paranoid that international mail wouldn't reach me, plastered each of her letters with a dozen stamps more than was needed. This habit had gotten worse with time, or perhaps she'd become all the more desperate to reach me in my newly motherless state. Inside the envelope was a lengthy message about my mom, how things were in Mexico, how everyone missed me and would love to host me again if I could get away from work.

Throughout my childhood, I spent every summer there.

My mom couldn't always afford to buy two plane tickets, so often it was just me and Mila. When Mila and I sat together on her porch, I would vent about how my friends in the States had probably forgotten me. Mila always knew just what to say—that *she* was also my friend and it was her duty to help make my stateside friends as jealous as possible. So, together, we wrote letters to them, detailing our shopping trips in Mexico City and our hikes around the volcano Popocatépetl. Of course, some of the details were exaggerated—a little extra extravagance, a little extra danger—but the letters achieved their aim. When I returned to the States, my friends always scrambled over to my house to ask about my adventures, their eyes bright and eager. It made me feel like a queen surrounded by her subjects.

Now, as I read Mila's letter addressed to me, I couldn't help but smile and soak in every word. Unlike the folks who texted me once, received my almost wordless response, and never reached out again, Mila went the extra mile with her message. It was long and detailed and, most importantly, didn't exude pity. When I arrived at the end, there was a piece of advice I couldn't ignore: "Take your auntie's word: Join a club. Find a community—something that isn't a grief group, something that makes you feel normal again. It's all part of the process, Lessi."

I hadn't been part of a club since I joined (and immediately un-joined) Future Business Leaders of America in high school. But as I folded up Mila's letter to put on my desk, I pondered her advice. Nothing had changed in the past four months. I still thought about Mom constantly, drank too much, and felt numb when I watched TV shows I used to love. Something more was needed to get me out of my slump, and as much as I bristled at the thought of human interaction—with the mailman, the grocery delivery driver, even the friends I'd made in college—Mila's wisdom had gotten me through plenty of hard times. It was best to give it a try.

So I checked Facebook for a community to join. Something local, preferably online. In-person hangouts might happen eventually, but for now, baby steps. Most groups didn't catch my interest: Omaha Adult Intramural Basketball, National Rifle Association–Omaha, Hobbytown Board Game Club. Sure, I could dribble a ball, shoot a gun, and kick my cousins' asses at Monopoly, but that didn't mean I wanted to dedicate myself to clubs in which those things were the sole focus. Over and over, I found people infinitely more passionate than I was doing things that would give me, at best, mild enjoyment.

Feeling as though I'd exhausted most of the local options —there were others farther away in Des Moines and KC—I sighed and closed my laptop. Mila's letter still rested on my desk, and I eyed it again. I couldn't give up on her advice so quickly. But I needed a break from the search, so I went to the kitchen to microwave some ramen. While the bowl filled up with water, I gazed out the window to my small backyard. Mom's gardening shed stood cobwebbed and rusting. The grass needed mowing, but as long as the city didn't issue me a warning and I wasn't going out anyway, I didn't see a reason to do it. Shading the grass was a crabapple tree with most of its pink blooms lost and browning in the prairie below.

A bird landed on the tree—a strange one I'd never seen before: a long black body with white wings, a red triangle on its head, and beady yellow eyes. It drilled the trunk with a white beak, *clack-clack-clack* like a toy soldier's gun.

And it occurred to me that the community I could be a part of was bird watchers. It wasn't that I had a passion for birds—especially when they sang me awake before sunrise— but I knew that bird watchers liked silence.

Taking out my phone, I snapped a picture of the bird, searched around until I found a Birds of Nebraska Facebook page, and posted my photo with the caption, "Can someone help ID? Seen in Omaha." I closed the app and finished making my ramen, figuring no one would reply.

———

I AWOKE to threats in my Facebook messages. Strangers calling me a "liar," "sick," and—in one especially memorable case—"a plague on the birding community." I didn't understand what I'd done, and even after I realized it was about the photo, the outrage still didn't make sense.

Thankfully, one kind soul gave me the benefit of the doubt, commenting, "Sorry, dear, but when was this picture taken? Ivory-billed woodpeckers have been extinct since the '80s. I'm sure you didn't mean to confuse folks!"

Extinct. I stared at that word for a long time, letting my Raisin Bran go soggy. But it wasn't long before I snapped into action. It'd been a long time since I'd "snapped" into anything. Was this what excitement felt like? Motivation? I wasn't sure, but I opened up my phone camera and hustled over to the kitchen window. Before I even got there, I heard the *clack-clack-clack*, and I knew the bird—the living fossil I now had a name for—was still there. But when I looked outside, there wasn't just one—there were two. A male and a female perhaps, drilling away at my crabapple tree to give their future babies a nest.

This time, I filmed it on Facebook live, narrating and getting multiple angles from different windows. I didn't dare step outside, though; no way I'd scare off my backyard miracle. Plus, I was just wearing underwear and a bra.

The online comments flooded in immediately. Some apologizing, others explaining how live videos could be faked ("she spray painted some pileated woodpeckers, I bet," "no, it's CG"). Countless more begging for the location in all caps. Somewhere around the hundredth demand for where I lived, the acid feeling in my chest became too uncomfortable to ignore. I stopped the livestream. Sure, documenting a supposedly extinct species was exciting, but my house becoming a bird tourist trap, thousands of binoculars peeking in on me from all directions? I couldn't stand the thought. I'd delete the post, claim it was an elaborate hoax, and get on with my quiet life. And while it would take some time for me to work up the courage again, I would still honor Mila's advice. A community would be good for me, but only one in which I could assert my personal boundaries.

Not a minute later, my "hoax" apology was posted, and I closed the app.

———

AROUND 3 P.M. that same day, I was in the middle of writing technical instructions for a Target-brand bookshelf when there was a knock at the door. Curious. I hadn't ordered any groceries, nor had I placed any Amazon orders in the past couple months. My best guess was that it might be a Jehovah's Witness or maybe a neighbor finally begging me to mow my lawn. But the man at the door wasn't wearing a white button-up with a tie, nor did he look like anyone I'd seen out walking their dogs or drinking on their porches. The first clue that this had gone too far was the man's binoculars hanging around his neck. Binoculars that looked fancy enough to match the price of a mid-sized sedan. The man was also sweating horribly, and his knocks grew more persistent the longer I watched through the sheer curtains.

"Please," he said. "I have to see them. It's—I never

thought it would happen. I didn't even think it was possible. I—I'll give you money, if you just let me in the backyard."

I didn't open the door, but I brushed the curtains aside. My voice trembled. "I don't want your money, and I don't want you in my yard," I said. "Please, just leave."

I caught the look in his eyes, dark, sunken, defeated. It was hard not to feel bad.

"But if you really have to," I continued, "just—just park in the alley and stand on top of your car. You should be able to see them over the fence."

Before I could even finish, he sprinted back to his car, cranked the ignition, and peeled into the alleyway. Immediately, I regretted ceding my ground. If the thousands of comments on my post were any indication, he wouldn't be the last to arrive.

I tried to ignore him and get the last of my work done for the day, going as far as to put on some noise-cancelling headphones and concentration-inducing alpha wave music. Still, my mind was jumbled, so it took me twice as long as it usually did to finish writing the bookshelf instructions. By five, I wasn't yet done, but five o'clock was five o'clock, so I called it quits, a headache blooming between my eyes. The next episode of *The Walking Dead* was a must, and maybe even some Chinese delivery. It had been a day.

But as soon as I took off the headphones, the outside world flooded in. Someone knocking at the door. Another person tapping at the window. Voices, some excited, others angry. Shushing—lots of shushing. And the constant *click-click-click* of cameras. The birdwatchers had arrived en masse, so many that apparently the "overflow" crowd wanted viewing space inside my house.

My breath caught in my throat, and I shoved my thumb in my mouth, gnawing at the nail—a habit I thought I'd broken. This wasn't what I wanted. Not in the least. And what could

I do? Yell at all those nerds? Call the cops? Shoot the damn birds? No, no. Each option was stressful in its own way. I wasn't an asshole, a fan of the boys in blue, or a psychopath. So what choice did that leave me with? Well, waiting for them to leave. Perhaps the birdwatchers would lose interest, or the woodpeckers would migrate elsewhere once they realized the innards of a crabapple tree were a bit cramped for their kin.

I prayed for it. Locked my bedroom door, closed the blinds, and clamped the noise-cancelling headphones back over my ears. It was almost like a sensory deprivation tank, except without the relaxation. My thoughts wouldn't stop, unspooling and tangling like a roll of toilet paper in a cat's paws. And not all the thoughts were rational: *What if the bird freaks never leave? What if they break in while I'm sleeping and claim squatters' rights? What if—?*

I couldn't live in this "whirlpool of worries," as Mom used to call it. And the second Mom sprung to mind, the tears flowed. I choked and sobbed and—when I worried that the birdwatchers might hear me—buried my face in a pillow. If Mom were here, she'd have rubbed my back, walked me to the kitchen, and brewed us each a cup of chamomile. When the cup was in my hand and at least halfway empty, then and only then would she ask me what was wrong. This ritual was better at calming me than any YouTube guided meditation video had ever been, and it broke my heart when Mom could no longer engage in it, too nerve-damaged to massage me or even flick the switch on her electric kettle. At least she still had her words, up until the very end. But now, even those were gone.

———

FALLING asleep that night was tough. Despite the curtains, light still bled in from the outside—camera flashes, mostly. The woodpeckers were apparently still on full display, though I didn't bother to check; I knew what they looked like already. It took four sleeping pills and an eye mask to finally lull me to sleep sometime after 2 a.m.

I forgot to set my alarm for work, but as it turned out, I didn't need it. I awoke to the sound of wings flapping and people gasping. The gasps didn't surprise me—these were "extinct" birds, after all. What did surprise me was the loudness of the flapping. It sounded less like two mates getting frisky and more like a whole flock swarming. I wrapped myself in a bathrobe and shuffled to the window, parting the curtain just an inch. I jerked back when a fast, white-tipped wing rustled the window screen from outside. And before I could close the curtain, another and another. Dozens of the "extinct" woodpeckers zipping around my yard, catching insects. Cameras clicked and bird watchers whispered, but their noises were buried behind those of the birds.

I looked at the wall clock, turned my face away, then looked again. If this were one of my lucid dreams, the clock might have read 2:15 one second and 10:38 the next, but the time was consistent. I was most certainly awake, under-caffeinated but heart beating as if the opposite were true.

It was time to take a window tour, not daring to actually step outside but rather acting as a voyeur who didn't wish to be seen, much less photographed. Moving from one window to the next, I could scarcely believe what I saw. Cars and news vans lined the block bumper to bumper, as if my house were the venue for a big pop concert. More expensive cameras than a red carpet event, and of course, woodpeckers in hordes. None of the birds seemed to move beyond my property line. None of them took up residence in my northern neighbor's more spacious oak tree, nor did they seem interested in my southern neighbor's bird feeder brimming with seeds. It was as if an invisible line marked their territory, and to cross it was to violate a law of nature.

As I stood staring, my phone rang. It was my Instacart delivery driver; I recognized his number even if I never answered his calls when he arrived with groceries. This time, however, I picked up, knowing there'd probably been a complication with the delivery.

"Hey, I, uh—it's impossible to get to your door," he said, the flapping of wings and clicking of cameras audible through the phone speaker. "I don't know if you know this, but there's—"

"Yeah, I know," I said, not meaning to come across short but doing so nonetheless. "Can you put the bags on the sidewalk? I'll—I can probably get to them from there."

"I don't know if you can, but, uh, sure."

A terrible taste spread across my tongue. Not normal morning breath, but something like old coffee grounds soaked in lemon juice. I took a deep breath, thanked the driver, and hung up. It was time to see if I could get outside.

As soon as I approached my front door, a cacophony of clacking greeted me. Not just one woodpecker, but countless, drilling away at the door. So many that the wood shuddered in its frame. I backed up, wondering how soon it would be before they bore their way into my home and made a nest in my living room. I held my breath, unsure what to do, before deciding I couldn't let it happen. I had to shoo them off, assert my boundaries, so I pounded against the door as if doing so might banish the birds back to extinction. But my pounding wasn't met with a flutter of fearful wings. No retreat at all, in fact. The birds hammered harder, faster. The door was not long for this world, and soon maybe I wouldn't be either.

I dialed Animal Control. If there was anyone who could

handle this situation without violence, it would be them. The phone rang six times before someone picked up, and I explained the situation.

"Yes," the woman on the line said, "we're well aware and have a team in front of your house already. It's an incredible sight, isn't it?"

I hung up without saying goodbye. What use was it? Nothing I could say would convince her of the danger I was in, the terror that rocked me. Hell, she'd probably been dreaming about something like this happening for ages. A birdwatcher's Christmas.

I was back at square one, waiting out the problem even as the swarm grew bigger by the second. The sound grew louder too. I could no longer distinguish between individual wing-beats and *clack-clack-clack*s. It was a thousand different rhythms playing simultaneously, blending into a seamless, deafening drone. And even when I put on the noise-cancelling headphones, the sound persisted like a bad case of tinnitus.

Again, I prayed, this time out loud, shouting myself hoarse. A prayer repeated over and over, sometimes addressed to God but more often to Mom. If she were here— in her room across the hall from mine—she would know what to do. Even if she couldn't fix the problem, she would have made bearing it so much easier, her words a sedative, quieter than the swarms but so much more powerful.

Around lunch time, I stopped praying, my throat feeling like hot copper. I needed a drink, some milk to soothe the burn. Yet the fridge was nearly empty. A jar of pickles, some salsa that had probably fermented by now, and two eggs a month past their expiration date. My groceries were still outside, or at least I hoped they were. Maybe the birds had crossed the property line and gotten to them. Or if not them, the bird watchers. My stomach rumbled, vacant and bubbling and sick all at once. I laid down on the kitchen floor, eyes closed, and waited for the feeling to subside.

Somehow, I fell asleep. Perhaps out of exhaustion, or maybe out of shock. I don't know. But when I awoke, there were ivory beaks poking out of the walls. Hundreds of them cheeping and thrashing their tongues, licking up wallpaper paste and pulverized plaster. I could no longer hear the sounds of the human world. No cameras clicking or cars pulling over or news reporters speaking into microphones with giddy disbelief. I couldn't see any people either—the windows were a mess of feathers and yellow eyes.

"What do you want?" I screamed, and their beaks opened and closed and unfurled tucked-away tongues.

Food. Maybe if I gave them food, they'd leave. But no way would I feed them by hand. Sure, I'd never heard of a man-eating bird, but I'd also never heard of ivory-billed woodpeckers until two days ago. I didn't know what they were capable of. I ran to Mom's room, hunting for the grabber she'd used to get clothes off their hangers. Her room was almost untouched, bed made, still smelling faintly of perfume and urine. The only difference was the holes in the wall with beaks jutting out. I snatched the grabber from her closet and ran back to the kitchen, opening up the pantry. Inside was an ancient box of saltine crackers, probably stale, but if birds could wolf down moldy bread, they probably wouldn't mind a stale cracker either.

I snapped each cracker in half and placed the pieces between the grabber's pincers. Then I held an offering out to each bird, one at a time. Sightless as they were, their eyes cloaked inside the walls, they sensed the food and snapped at it, crumbs falling to the floor but most of the cracker sliding down their gullets in a single gulp. Still, the ones I fed didn't retreat. If anything, they grew more restless, beaks slapping against the sides of their holes.

What was I to do? I wept. I begged for Mom—her spirit, her rotted body, her clothes animated to imitate her form. I didn't care. All I knew was that I couldn't do this alone. Without her strength, I'd end up dying. Screaming pleas shredded my vocal cords.

And then the birds stopped cheeping, stopped thrashing around inside the walls. My tears ceased. Something was happening. A moment later, thousands of wings beat, not as a wall of chaotic noise, but as a unified rhythm. A rumble shook the floor. Concrete cracked. A whoosh of wind blew up through the floorboards and I lost my balance, the grabber flying out of my hand. Vertigo hit me hard. A wave of dizziness so intense I retched. There was nothing in my stomach —just a thick slither of bile.

When I found my footing, I walked over to the kitchen window as if on a tightrope, bending at the knees to keep from falling. The window was still blocked by a cluster of feathers and eyes, but through a crack I could see only the sky. Not a single building or tree or human. The color darkened the higher up we got, from pale blue to navy to almost black. My breath thinned, and even as the floor steadied itself, my vertigo intensified. I sat down, counted my inhales and exhales.

Sometime around my thousandth breath, I realized I was no longer on the floor. I was floating, just an inch or two, but still—floating. So too were my fridge, my stack of bills, and Mom's jar of old pesos. Again, I retched, but this time the bile floated with me, spittle parting from my chin and levitating away.

The wing beats grew quieter until they were silent—no sound in space. Still, I sensed we were moving, moving far faster than I thought birds capable of, this migration a cosmic one. I wondered for a moment if I was already dead. I grabbed a steak knife suspended in air and poked my finger, digging in until I drew blood. A crimson drop floated away like a planet falling out of orbit. So, I was alive. But how? And for how much longer?

I used the drifting fridge to propel myself to the window, gripping a curtain rod to stay in place. Once more, I found the crack between the feathers and unblinking eyes, and I peered into the blackness.

Except the blackness wasn't pure. There was something far off. Lights. No, stars. *A ring of stars.* Golden and growing nearer each moment. A tingling warmth spread through my chest and flowed into my extremities. A weight lifted from both body and soul, as absent as gravity. I laughed a sound-less laugh, terrified, ecstatic.

———

WE'RE GETTING CLOSER NOW. I don't know how long it's been, but I'm coming, Mom. I'll be there soon.

GRAY MATTER

"You know we found bits of him, right?" the cop says. "Forensics is still figuring out exactly what those bits are, but they don't look like his outsides. You know anything about that?"

Asim sits in the interrogation room, still wearing his scrubs. The AC is broken—or maybe the officers turned it off—so he's already sweat through his clothes several times over in the four hours he's been here.

Amirah sits across from him. She's dressed for her adult softball tournament, but Asim's call pulled her away right before she stepped up to the plate. Amirah turns to the cops, taking a legal pad and pen out of her saddle bag.

"Will you give me and my client some time, please?" she asks.

The male cop rolls his eyes, and the female cop mutters something under her breath, but both leave, locking the door behind them. There's a moment of thick silence, then Amirah leans in toward Asim.

"I'm missing a game for this," she says. "Your sister's pissed."

"I know," Asim says, and he starts crying.

"Shit, Asim. I was trying to lighten the mood, not—"

She sighs, then pulls an eyeglass cloth out of her bag to wipe Asim's cheeks. Asim twists his head as if to deny his tears are there, but at Amirah's touch he relaxes. After Amirah finishes, she puts the cloth back in her bag, then clicks her pen.

"You don't have to tell me if you did it—"

"I didn't," Asim says, shaking his wrists in the too-tight cuffs.

"Okay, but I need to be able to defend you. Tell me what happened, from the beginning. Your version of the story."

"You're not going to believe me."

"Your sister's paying me to believe you."

"Fuck," Asim says, and he puts his head on the table— bangs it once but not hard enough to bruise.

When he lifts it back up, he cracks his neck and glances back up at the clock. 4:06. He'll be late to work if he tells the whole story, but doing so might also keep him out of prison —or land him in an asylum. Either way, he doesn't have much choice.

He takes a deep breath and begins.

———

MR. PERSSON probably would've ended up in assisted living if his children visited more often. They had the cash to pay for it—Emma being a radiologist and Ari a pediatrician—but I've never seen them visit. In fact, I might have been Mr. Persson's only visitor in the six months since his wife died. It was my job to help the man with his medication, do whichever chores were beyond his ability, and ask him about his interests. It wasn't that I particularly liked talking about

Clive Cussler novels or old Swedish films. It was more that encouraging the man to access his knowledge of those things would help preserve the memories longer. After Mrs. Persson's death, Mr. Persson's mind started unspooling like a fishing rod with a whale on the other end. Nothing could reverse the process, but certain measures could slow it down. In addition to encouraging trips down a crumbling memory lane, I sometimes did crosswords with Mr. Persson. When crosswords eventually proved too much for the man, we went to word searches instead. Still, a word I found in three seconds would take Mr. Persson ten times as long to find. But it didn't matter. As long as I was on the clock, I could wait.

One morning a few months back, I was at Mr. Persson's house after a long night of gaming with friends. I hadn't slept much, but Mr. Persson and I were comfortable enough with each other that he didn't mind if we took a mid-morning nap at the same time. There I was, lying on his couch, which was about a foot too short and a little musty but comfortable enough. Mr. Persson had popped in a DVD of some classic Swedish film to teach me the language, but the black-and-white picture and subtitles were enough to make me feel my lack of sleep. The man was in the bathroom, so I figured I could close my eyes until he came back without causing offense. As I drifted, a sound plucked me back into consciousness. I wasn't sure if it was a dream or something real, but it sounded like Mr. Persson was whispering. I opened my eyes and sat up. The sound was coming from the bathroom, so I went to investigate, hoping the man hadn't fallen or pissed himself before reaching the toilet.

When I opened the bathroom door, Mr. Persson was kneeling in front of the toilet like a sick-drunk college student, but he wasn't puking his guts out. He was whispering into the bowl, his bony fingers trembling on the rim.

"Min älskling," he said, "är du där?"

I knew that "min älskling" meant "my love." He'd taught me that in case I ever met a pretty Swedish girl. We hadn't quite broached my whole asexual thing yet, but still, the language lesson proved useful here. I felt a pang seeing the man whisper those words into the toilet. Dementia made people do strange things, and I'd hoped this stage wouldn't come so soon.

"Mr. Persson," I said, bending down and holding out my hand to him.

He turned his face toward me slowly. A stray pube clung to his chin from resting it on the toilet rim, but he smiled, totally unaware.

"She's here," he said. "She's back."

A shiver ran through me, and I tried to compose myself the only way I knew how—moving on without comment. I grabbed a wad of toilet paper and wiped off Mr. Persson's chin. He frowned and grumbled a Swedish goodbye as I lowered the toilet seat.

"Do you want to keep watching the movie?" I asked, helping the man up.

"Nej," he replied. "I'm not in the mood."

"I thought you loved Ingo Bergman."

"Ing*mar*," he corrected.

He gazed longingly at the toilet once more, and I didn't know whether to laugh or get the hell out of there. Neither option was terribly professional, so I instead escorted the man out into the living room. The whole time, I pictured those toilets in Australia that become home to ten-foot-long snakes hiding in the pipes. Not älskling material, if you ask me.

———

"SOUNDS like you and this guy got along okay," Amirah says. "Too bad about his dementia—really changes a person."

"Oh, you have no idea," Asim says, massaging his temples.

———

IT'S no surprise that plenty of old people still have sex drives. The ones who have a partner and the ability to have sex do it, and the ones who have no one still masturbate. Mr. Persson would sometimes excuse himself for that very purpose, and I knew what he was doing, but it didn't bother me. Thing is, he was normally good at cleaning up after himself, but this one day was different. I think it was a week after the toilet incident. He left for the bathroom like normal, grinning and glancing over his shoulder at me as he hobbled across the carpet. I put my headphones in, figuring I'd give the man some sonic privacy. But three EDM tracks in, his voice cut through the music. It was a cry, but I couldn't tell if it was one of pleasure or pain. I tore my headphones out and dashed to the bathroom, whipping open the door without knocking.

Mr. Persson was sitting on the toilet, clothed in only a sweater. A black ooze coated his waist, and at first I thought he'd had an accident, but whatever it was, it had a sharp, synthetic smell like diesel. The man had an erection, and my initial thought was that he'd used something as lube that wasn't supposed to be lube. This happens sometimes with dementia patients—well, not the lube thing specifically, but mistaking one item for another; a tube of itch cream for a tube of toothpaste, for instance.

"Sorry for interrupting, Mr. Persson," I said, averting my eyes while still speaking through a crack in the door. "Do you need any help?"

"She's as good in the sack now as she was then, Asim," he said, and he laughed.

Getting up from the toilet, he slipped on a glob of the ooze that had fallen to the tile, but thankfully he landed right back on the toilet seat. I opened the door and rushed over.

"Please, let me help you," I said, gesturing for him to stay seated.

As I cleaned up the mess, Mr. Persson kept chuckling to himself, peeking below him into the toilet, muttering incoherent flirtations. I glanced around the bathroom to see if I could find whatever the hell he'd gotten all over himself. The trash can was full of used tissues, bloodied floss, and dulled shaving razors, but nothing out of the ordinary. I didn't find anything strange in the medicine cabinet either—pills and toothpaste, mostly. With no obvious answers in sight, it was best to ask the man directly.

"Mr. Persson, what is this stuff, anyway?"

"Oh," he said, shaking his head and laughing until he coughed. "Don't tell me you've never gotten a woman excited."

"Never mind," I said, pulling the man's pants over his legs. "Lift your feet, please."

When Mr. Persson was fully cleaned and dressed, I helped him out of the bathroom. His pace was slow as he shuffled across the floor in his slippers, but he hummed a bouncy tune. This was the first time I'd ever heard him get musical, and I smiled a bit despite the circumstances.

Then came a gurgle from the bathroom. I glanced behind me just as a tiny spout of gray water splashed out of the toilet, like a dolphin clearing its blowhole. Mr. Persson turned his head, kissed his hand, and blew the kiss into the bathroom.

As soon as we got to the living room couch, he asked me

to put on Turner Classic Movies, saying the TV remote was too confusing to operate himself. I turned on the TV, then checked my phone, counting the minutes until I could run out the front door.

———

AMIRAH HASN'T BOTHERED to write anything in her notepad for the past several minutes. She's too busy staring at Asim, knitting her eyebrows.

"Hey," Asim says. "You got any water? They haven't given me—"

"So, let me get this straight," Amirah says, blowing past the question. "Mr. Persson was a horndog with dementia. How this is connected to—"

"I promise it'll make sense soon. Do you have water?"

Amirah pulls a half-full water bottle out of her saddle bag, unscrews the lid, and hands it to Asim. He drinks all of it, breathing heavily after the last drop slides down his throat. Amirah sighs, then speaks.

"You were saying?"

———

OVER THE NEXT FEW WEEKS, Mr. Persson made jokes less and asked to be left alone more. He spent most of his time looking through family photo albums, but instead of smiling down at pictures of his loved ones he grumbled under his breath and scratched his liver-spotted head. Sometimes, when he thought I wasn't looking, he'd hold a photo up and point it toward the bathroom door.

"I'm forgetting this one," he'd say. "Jog my memory, älskling."

Sometimes the toilet would gurgle in response, and in those moments I'd scurry off to some far corner of the house, claiming there was a chore that had to be done urgently. I'd dust the attic with my headphones playing full blast to avoid hearing what I could no longer pass off as a strange plumbing issue. And when it came time to return downstairs, I had to do breathing exercises to prepare for it, bouncing in place and puffing out my cheeks like a runner before a big race. Sometimes these pump-up sessions even delayed Mr. Persson's medication schedule.

But I was not entirely negligent of my duties. I don't want you to get the wrong idea, especially given the circumstances under which I'm telling you this story. When it counted—and I mean *really* counted—I did everything in my power to keep Mr. Persson safe.

It was one of those days when I found a random chore to do without the man even asking me—washing the curtains, in this case. They smelled okay and weren't even all that dusty, but I took any excuse I could find to get far away from the bathroom. Just as I was pulling them out of the washer, a scream erupted from downstairs. I froze, wondering if the man was having a heart attack, but I didn't hear his body thud to the floor. Instead, I heard a sound like wet hissing. Mr. Persson had a deep voice and a perpetually dry mouth, so I couldn't imagine the sound coming from him, but I also had no idea who else it could come from; we were alone in the house.

I rushed downstairs, wiping my moist, detergent-scented hands off on my scrubs. When I burst into the living room, Mr. Persson was pinching a rusty nail between two fingers and holding it to his forehead, a drizzle of blood snaking down the bridge of his nose. In his other hand, he held a hammer. I dove for the hammer like I was diving for home base, knocking him off balance as I snatched it. He wind-milled his hands for a moment, dropping the nail, then landed on the couch with an "oof." Once he caught his breath, he looked at me the same way TSA agents do. His cheeks were flushed and twitching, and had I not taken a step back, he might have swung at me.

"I was making room for her," he said, a gob of spit clinging to his chapped lips.

"You were hurting yourself," I replied, not at all following. "You're bleeding,"

My fingers clamped together repeatedly as I searched for a tissue. I found one, but as I reached to wipe the blood from his chin, he grabbed my wrist with surprising force. He leaned forward, his breath smelling like an oil spill. When he bared his teeth at me, black ooze clung to his receding gums—the same substance I'd seen on him in the bathroom weeks back.

"She'll help me remember," he said, snatching the tissue, wadding it up, and tossing it to the carpet.

The redness emptied from the man's face. Paler than ever before, he glanced around the room, blinking repeatedly. When his eyes landed back on me, he smiled.

"Do you want to watch a movie, Asim?" he asked.

I opened my mouth but didn't know what to say, so I grabbed a blanket from the recliner, put it over the man's lap, and turned on the TV until he fell asleep. It wasn't five minutes before he was snoring, all his energy expended in the outburst. When I was sure he was asleep, I cleaned his head wound. Despite the sting of peroxide, he didn't even stir, his head lulling to the right and the waddle of his chin fluttering with each snore.

I called his kids while I had the chance, looking over my shoulder every few seconds to make sure he hadn't woken up and nailed his brains into oblivion. I spoke with Emma first, then Ari, but neither conversation went anywhere.

"Oh, Dad was probably just messing around," Emma said.

"I'm sure it was a joke," Ari echoed.

When both ended the call with, "Listen, I've got a lot of work here," I took a picture of Mr. Persson's head wound to send their way, feeling like a creep as I snapped close-ups of the dozing man. Neither Emma nor Ari responded. After giving them another half-hour to reply, I cursed at my phone and chucked it at the recliner. The soft *whoomp* was enough to wake Mr. Persson. He let out a loud snort and jerked his head upward. Immediately, every muscle in my body tightened. The man looked around, blinking and clutching the couch cushion as if it were a flotation device and the living room an ocean.

"Where am I?" he asked, though not to me.

I was frozen in place like a rabbit in the presence of a wolf, camouflaged at least for now. I didn't realize I'd been holding my breath, but when I finally exhaled, the man snapped his head in my direction.

"Oh," he said. "Is this your home?"

The tension in my body eased. I hadn't seen Mr. Persson this out of it before, but the delusion that this was my house was much easier to manage than the delusion that a nail through the skull would bring back lost memories. I didn't correct Mr. Persson for that exact reason, certain that reminding him he owned this house would also remind him of his plan to self-mutilate. There comes a time when you stop correcting dementia patients' delusions; it only gives them that foggy, far-off look in their eyes as they grasp for a reality that died inside them long ago.

With that in mind, I sat beside Mr. Persson and put on a movie. Not one that I liked, but one that he'd comfort-watched a dozen times—*Stagecoach*. Mr. Persson watched with rapt attention as if this were his first time seeing it. Perhaps, in a sense, it was.

————

"WHAT'S THAT LOOK FOR?" Asim asks from across the interrogation table. "The cops were giving me that same look."

"Sorry," Amirah says, leaning back in her chair and scratching the back of her head. "I just . . . where is this going? I don't understand."

"Neither do I. Not really. And like I said, you're probably not going to believe me."

"Well, let's get to the part I won't believe. I think the cops are getting impatient."

Asim eyes the metal door and sees the male cop staring through the glass, chewing on a vending-machine cinnamon roll.

"Is this room soundproof?" Asim asks.

"Privacy, please!" Amirah says, widening her eyes and waving her hand at the onlooker.

The cop smirks, takes a massive bite of his cinnamon roll, and walks away.

"It's just you and me now," Amirah says, turning back to Asim.

"All right. Let's wrap this shit up."

————

SINCE MR. PERSSON'S kids were out of the picture, I called the care agency to see what they could do for him. The transition to more intensive care would take at least a week, but when I repeatedly mentioned the hammer incident, they said they'd get him in sooner—assuming the proper paperwork was signed. In the meantime, my shifts would be longer than normal, me pulling double duty with caretaking and suicide watch.

The first day—yesterday—was mostly uneventful. Mr. Persson wandered room to room, looking at picture frames on the wall. The pictures showed his children in their school days, but they might as well have been stock photo models. He squinted at them, his throat wheezing with each shallow breath. Not once did a smile creep onto his face, and I didn't bother reminding him who the people were; I doubted he'd believe me. Instead, I just followed him, room to room to room, until we were back in the same place we started. It was like a never-ending merry-go-round.

"I'm empty," Mr. Persson said, over and over.

When the end of my shift came, I put the man to bed and got the hell out of there, a night of video games, Chinese takeout, and a few too many beers calling my name. Maybe drinking myself to sleep would erase the memory of the day —a memory that had already probably vanished from Mr. Persson's mind without the aid of booze. But given that I'm telling you all this now, my efforts to forget it all failed.

I woke up the next morning—this morning—with a throbbing headache. After vomiting up a stomach full of chow mein, chugging a glass of water, and throwing up the glass of water, I pulled on some clothes and drove to Mr. Persson's house. I was five minutes late, and I wonder if he'd still be alive if I hadn't drunk myself sick. That's not to say he's dead, but we'll get to that in a minute.

When I entered his home, a sharp smell immediately assaulted my senses. It was a mix of both that familiar burning-oil smell and something like an industrial cleaner. I looked around the living room and saw no sign of Mr. Persson, but a dripping sound came from the bathroom. I approached the closed door slowly. I should've done the opposite, but I couldn't push my feet to go any faster. The closer I got, the clearer I heard whatever was happening in the bathroom—not only the dripping, but also a faint fizzing. Without knowing what it was, the sound still made my gut turn even though I had nothing left to puke. I hesitated, then turned the doorknob. The door creaked open an inch at a time, and when I could finally see what was happening inside, it took me several seconds to process the sight. Of course, I'm still processing it now. Describing it feels like describing a nightmare, or a fucked-up hallucination.

Mr. Persson had his head tilted to the side above the toilet. He held a bottle of liquid plumber above him and poured it into his ear at a steady drizzle. His eyes twitched periodically but otherwise had an iron focus, the sharpness of his younger self shining through the cataracts. The fizzing was coming from inside him, liquid plumber bubbling at the rims of his ear like a hot spring. When it spilled over the edges and down his cheek, he stopped the drizzle and let the liquid burn its way inside him. It was then that my stomach found something—however small or sticky—to expel. I retched, bile dripping down my chin as I stumbled toward the man, one hand against the wall to keep my balance. But I stopped just as soon, seeing the liquid drain out the other ear, a hole burned all the way through. Impossibly, Mr. Persson lifted his head and lowered the bottle. Viewing him in profile, I saw something inside his ear—the other side of the wall, bathroom tile reflecting yellowed light. The sight was enough to make me fall back, but what came next made me fucking cower.

Creeping around the side of his head and clinging to what little gray hair remained, a black creature slithered into view. It clung to him, round like a tick but with suckers instead of legs. I opened my mouth to scream, and no sound escaped.

"Make me whole, älskling," Mr. Persson said, his voice clear and bright.

And just as the thing slithered into his ear, contracting its slug-like body to fit, I passed the fuck out.

I don't know how long it was before I woke up, but when I did, Mr. Persson was gone—nowhere to be found in his house. There were drippings of what I assume was his brain on the bathroom floor and on the carpet leading to the open front door, but the trail disappeared after that. I screamed his name repeatedly and ran around the block searching, my head throbbing with pressure, but he was gone.

He's still gone.

———

AMIRAH HAS a hand over her mouth. She's already turned away from Asim.

"I'm sorry," Asim says. "I told you that you wouldn't believe me."

"It's sick, Asim," Amirah replies, only looking at him through her peripherals. "You have a fucked-up imagination."

Asim places his head on the cold interrogation table. He would cry, but he doesn't have anything left in him. He's going to prison, and he knows it.

Then, the door opens and the male cop walks in. Amirah whips around and stands up, trying to hide the sickly look on her face.

"What did I say about giving me time alone with my client?" she says.

"Your client has a visitor," the cop says, a sour, almost disappointed look on his face. "And your client is a free man."

Asim lifts his head, blinking several times to make sure this is real. "What do you mean?" he asks.

"Mr. Persson is here to see you. Turns out he's fine, after all. Chipper, even."

Asim's breath catches inside him, and his head jerks back and forth between the cop and Amirah.

"Close the door," he says, his words coming out choked and small.

"What?" the cop asks.

"For the love of God, don't let that thing in."

SICK LEAVE

When Truc stumbled into work in a sweat-soaked polo and a cough that could be heard all the way in aisle 32, I was pissed. Not because she "lacked professionalism," as our supervisor Rochelle sometimes claimed, but because she called in sick and our boss Mr. Davis told her "no." End of conversation. She'd texted me an expletive-laden account of the exchange on her way over.

While scanning a customer's paint cans, I watched Truc shuffle to her register and hack up a lung all over the keyboard. I shook my head, unaware that my current customer—a man in a Hard Rock Café shirt—was thrusting a coupon in my face. When the man snapped his fingers at me, I whipped my head in his direction, apologized, and applied the 20% discount. He hadn't been the first customer to literally snap in my ear at High's Hardware.

Out of the corner of my eye, I noticed Rochelle stomping over to Truc's register with her hands perched on her hips.

"You're five minutes late," she said. "This is your second warning, Tran."

I cringed. Not only was Rochelle indifferent to Truc's

deathly illness, she was also racist as hell, frequently mixing up the names of the two Vietnamese employees who worked here—the other one being me. Truc corrected her most of the time, but today she seemed too exhausted to deal with that shit. I couldn't blame her.

Behind me, Truc's cough snowballed into something even more phlegmy, wheezy, and asthmatic than before. It went on long enough that even Hard Rock Café guy took notice, pulling his sunglasses down an inch to get a better look.

"Quit that—you're disturbing the customers," Rochelle said to Truc, like a parent to a misbehaving child.

I told the customer his total, whispering so the outburst I was trying to contain wouldn't come out. The man squinted down at the chip reader and put in his PIN number.

Truc's coughing fit slowed to a halt, and she breathed a few long, ragged breaths. Rochelle waited with her arms folded one over the other. What came out of Truc's mouth next left an expression for the history books on Rochelle's face.

"This is bullshit," Truc said. "I'm talking to the boss. Tran?"

As soon as I heard my name, I jerked my head around. The customer's receipt had already printed, but when he realized I wasn't going to hand it to him, he reached over the counter and ripped it off himself.

"Yeah?" I said, my heartbeat quickening as I stole a glance at the red-faced Rochelle.

Truc coughed again, wiping a string of saliva off her chin, then said, "Will you go with me?"

Rochelle raised an eyebrow in my direction, as if whatever I did next would be the difference between an overdue raise and a pink slip. I bit my lip, hesitated a moment, then nodded at Truc. Rochelle made a performatively loud scoff and gestured at the next customer in my line. But it didn't matter. I had to help my friend.

"I am so, so sorry," Rochelle said to the customer, her words like razors slicing the air.

Truc and I walked away from the registers and through the PVC plumbing aisle on our way to the warehouse. A customer tried to stop us with questions about a price, but when I told her Truc was about to vomit—it could've been true from the way she was hunched over—the man grimaced and backed away, muttering that he'd find someone else.

"Thank you," Truc whispered. "I'm sorry if I get you fired."

"No, it's all good," I said as we passed through the stainless-steel double doors into the warehouse. "Mr. Davis shouldn't have made you come in."

"His office is back here, right?"

Truc coughed like a forty-year smoker. For a moment I thought she might collapse, but she waved her hand dismissively and continued walking. We wandered past rows and rows of wooden pallets and storage shelves as tall as two-story houses. The warehouse seemed bigger than the shop floor itself. Given that our shifts began right as the stocking crew's ended, we rarely came back here. But Truc had covered shifts for the stockers, many of whom had called in sick with the same thing as Truc, received Mr. Davis's "no" for an answer, and stayed home anyway. Good for them.

"You know what bugs me?" Truc said, clearing the mucus from her throat. "Mr. Davis is never out on the floor with us. I've never seen him. I mean, Rochelle's who hired and trained me, and she barely does shit except yell at us, but"—she launched into another coughing fit—"but Davis *literally* does nothing, from what I can tell."

"You think I didn't notice?" I said, then paused to take in my surroundings.

It was darker the farther we got into the warehouse. High above us, rows of dim fluorescent lights swung gently in air-conditioned currents. It was colder back here too. I shivered but didn't have a sweater to put on over my blue work vest. The only sound was the background hum of central air, and when I squinted at the rows of shelves ahead, they seemed to continue without end—a one-point perspective drawing where the opposite sides of a road appear to meet on the horizon.

"Jesus," Truc said, breathing hard and dragging her feet. "How big is this place? I've never been back this far. We better find Davis's office before I crash."

"What do you plan to tell him, anyway?" I asked, but my attention was split, more focused on how cavernous the warehouse was than what Truc was saying.

I glanced behind me to make sure we could still see the exit, those double doors now pinprick-small in the distance.

"I just want him to know that it was fucked-up to make me come in today," Truc said, taking a moment to sniffle and gag. "And that I deserve a raise for coming in, anyway."

"Shit, even if you didn't come in, you'd still deserve a raise. We all deserve one," I said, then stopped in place. "Hey, are you sure we didn't overshoot the office? It's just— it's really dark over that way and . . . I dunno."

"No, I mean, I don't see any doors back that way. Just . . . lots of shelves. Continue on, I guess?"

I hesitated, then nodded, pulling out my phone to use as a flashlight. Most of the overhead lights in this part of the warehouse had burned-out, and the few that still functioned flickered on and off. From the glow of my phone, I could see that the shelves back here were mostly empty. On one, there was an open box of old, rusted nails. On another sat a sandwich, half-eaten and gray with mold. Cobwebs stretched from shelf to shelf like ghostly bunting.

"This place gives me the creeps," I said.

"Me too," Truc said, her words getting quieter and her pitch higher as she stifled a cough. "Can you shout for him? Maybe he'll come out."

Having held it in as long as she could, she let out a nasty series of throat-rending coughs, propping her hand against one of the shelves so she wouldn't fall over. She pulled it away just as soon, wiping wispy strands of cobwebs off on her vest.

"Mr. Davis!" I shouted as loud as I could.

My call cascaded through the warehouse but, like a rock dropped down a bottomless well, returned no echo. I realized my breath was visible, misty white and rising toward a ceiling I could no longer see. My foot involuntarily tapped the unswept concrete floor, and I turned around to check for the exit. It wasn't there. Or at least, it was too distant to make out. The overhead lights behind us had begun to die, too, one by one, a uniform dimness cloaking the chamber. Pungent mold spores floated in front of my phone light, riding a sluggish current.

"This is fucked-up," I whispered, as if someone other than Truc might hear me.

Truc stood still, staring up at the ceiling and swaying back and forth as if she were drunk. Her eyes twitched and watered. Her breathing sounded like wind whistling through a cracked window.

"Truc, are you okay?" I asked, already knowing the answer.

She lay down on the floor, her cheeks puffing out with each soft cough.

From the darkness came a screech of metal against concrete, distant but close enough to make my heart leap. I gazed into the gloom until Truc spoke, apparently unaware of the sound.

"I need to rest," she said, her words slurring together as she closed her eyes.

"No, no," I replied, reaching for her hand as she lay down. "Not now. Get up. We'll—we'll go back to the shop floor and . . . and we'll send Mr. Davis a complaint email. We'll, uh, have all the other cashiers sign off on it. 'Paid sick days now!' Yeah, yeah . . . how's that sound? Truc? Truc?"

But Truc was asleep, her chest rising and falling just barely. If it weren't for her soft snoring, I would have thought she was dead. She might've been close to that point, though. Who knew what the hell kind of disease she had? It had lingered for weeks, that vile mucus thickening inside her each day, but she didn't have the money to get diagnosed and treated. The stockers were probably just as ill as Truc, if not more so, and we hadn't heard from them in a while. If they were dead, I doubted Rochelle would even tell us.

"Fuck," I said, dropping Truc's limp hand and looking around.

One of the ancient shelves beside me leaned against another like a falling domino frozen in time. A layer of dust an inch thick coated its surface. On the floor below was a handsaw, long and red with what I hoped was rust. The mold, earthy and rotten, hung in the air, and I wondered if Truc passed out from inhaling it, blankets of spores clinging to her lungs like black velvet.

I picked her up and was about to haul her back to the shop floor when an inhuman voice, low and gravelly, cut through the darkness. It seemed to come from all directions at once.

"Your lunch break is only thirty minutes, girls," it said. "Better get back to work."

I nearly dropped Truc, catching her before her head could hit the concrete. After lowering her gently to the ground, I spun in a circle, illuminating what little of the space my phone light could reach. No one was there. Just the tall shelves looming overhead like dead iron gods.

"Mr. Davis," Truc mumbled, though I couldn't tell if she was conscious or sleep talking. Her eyelids fluttered but didn't open, and after lolling her head to one side, she settled into a statue-like stillness.

Then came a creak from atop a shelf. I snapped my head upward in time to see the black silhouette crouched high above, humanoid in shape and with eyes glowing a primal green. Even through the darkness, I could make out its extraordinary height, the shelf dipping under its weight. But before I could get a better look, the creature scrambled away on all fours, muscled shoulders rising and falling with each bound.

Despite my better instincts, I followed, trying not to breathe in the musty spores as I ran. I only made it so far before the air inside me boiled and I had to release it, panting for more. A taste as bitter as oil filled my mouth, but I kept running. The creature outpaced me, and as its feet slammed against the crumbling shelf, bits of rust rained down and falling glass jars exploded at my feet, splattering me with liquid that smelled at once medicinal and toxic. My tennis shoes squished into the contents of the jars—something slimy and firm, but yielding. I didn't dare look to see what it was.

When the creature reached the end of the shelf, it leapt at the wall. I was still a ways behind, my soaked, glass-splintered shoes slowing me down. I thought the creature would fall and break its legs, but it grabbed onto an open air vent with a deafening metallic bang, easing itself in and then closing the grate. The groan of steel straining beneath its body continued for a minute before the sound dissipated. The creature was gone, at least for now. I stood below the vent, gasping for breath and unable to move.

Somewhere behind me came another screech, probably metal dragging across concrete again, but it almost sounded like a mountain lion's scream—a sound I'd heard once while camping and never wanted to hear again. I shuddered. Remembering Truc, I ran to where I'd left her, hoping she might be the one responsible for the noise.

When I got there, she was nowhere to be seen, the shape of her body an imprint in the dust. I saw no footprints leading farther into the warehouse, nor did I see any heading back toward the shop floor. My heart palpitated, arrhythmic and violent.

"Truc!" I screamed.

I called again and again, her name transforming into pain in my throat.

I searched the area for what felt like hours, never straying too much farther into the warehouse and always keeping an eye out for the creature. After a while, I heard a shelf clatter to the ground. I sprinted over to investigate. From what I could tell, the shelf had collapsed in on itself, so old and rusted that something as small as a breeze could have reduced it to rubble. There was no sign that the creature was responsible—no oversized footprints in the dust, no scurrying sounds of retreat. I dug through the mess, hoping I'd find Truc buried there and still breathing. Crusted metal shards bit into my hands. The pain barely registered, blood and orange rust streaking my arms like a sunset. But Truc was nowhere to be found. Worse yet, there were only minutes of battery left on my phone light.

A cough was brewing inside me, and not just from all my yelling. When it came out, it sounded like a car engine sputtering to life, a dozen short, dry chokes leading up to a roar. I didn't need a doctor to know I'd caught what Truc had. Swiftly descending, this sickness weighed down my eyelids, inflicting me with fatigue and tempting me with sleep. But I resisted, wandering the warehouse in a daze, rasping out Truc's name between coughing spells. My eyes grew heavier by the second, and despite my resistance, I drifted in and out of consciousness mid-step. When my eyes opened again, my phone light was out, sending a jolt through my spine, but the darkness lulled me into a walking sleep again seconds later. Each time I slipped back into consciousness, I found myself in an entirely different part of the warehouse, blind but reading the surroundings through my remaining senses: the chittering of bats; the itch of stagnant water drenching me up to my calves; the smell of smoke where there was no fire.

After what must have been my thousandth bout of accidental sleepwalking, I wound up back at the double doors leading to the shop floor. I blinked several times to make sure I wasn't hallucinating. But the marathon-runner ache in my legs was too painful to be my imagination. Through the grubby windows were customers browsing a deck chair display that didn't look familiar. I passed through the doors, zombielike and squinting. The light burned my eyes.

Just as my vision cleared, Rochelle walked past me, then stopped and backtracked. She looked at me hard, as if she almost recognized me but not quite. Something was different about the woman, her high bun now streaked with gray, the logo on her work vest sleeker and more simplified than the one on mine, her eyes more tired than angry.

"Do I—?" she started, then shook her head.

She rushed away before I had a chance to say anything. And really, what could I have said? What would have changed anything?

I closed my eyes, and all I could see were rows of rusted shelves receding into infinity.

THE PATCH

Vince has never ridden a seaplane before, and given his tendency toward both air and seasickness, it's not something he'd like to do again. Of course, he'll have to ride it back to Hawaii when the job is over, but the queasiness is worth it, given that he's finally writing for the *Forbes* "30 Under 30" list after years of shitting out listicles for a third-rate entrepreneur blog.

But right now, Vince is on the verge of losing his lunch—a room-temperature tuna sandwich—as the plane descends through a rain cloud. The pilot crackles in through Vince's headset, promising "some light turbulence but a smooth landing." Saorise Walsh sits beside Vince, gazing out the window with an expressionless face. She's probably been on hundreds of flights just like this one and is no longer moved by the majesty and terror of air travel. No surprise she's wearing her own brand—"Sustain," athleisure made from the Great Pacific Garbage Patch's plastic stew, promising "breathability, durability, and sustainability," but it's out of Vince's price range until this *Forbes* paycheck comes in. The emerald green workout shirt looks good on Walsh. Matches her hair—red, silky, hanging down to her waist without the least bit of frizz. There's also a sea turtle tattoo on her left hand. Neat.

They're silent now, but Vince and Saorise talked for the first hour of the flight, got some of the preliminary interview questions out of the way. Ones about her youth—only child, raised in a McMansion—and the company's origins. Her dad's a rich liberal congressman who lent Saorise the startup capital for Sustain. Just two years later, there are rumors about the company going global. Walsh won't confirm it, but she smiled when Vince asked. Of course, as a journalist, Vince can't infer fact from a smile. Still, it's clear Walsh is doing well for herself. Doing well for the world, too, ostensibly, if turning junk into yoga pants for rich people counts.

The plane is about to land. It broke through the clouds a minute ago, and the ocean is visibly churning below. Vince thinks he's gonna puke.

VINCE MIGHT NOT UNDERSTAND how the Sea Sweeper works, but the machine is impressive. It's like a whale-sized vacuum, sucking in garbage and storing it in detachable crates ready for transport—six tons of non-organic material each hour. "Non-organic" is Walsh's wording. She's still in damage control mode after that *New York Times* hit job claimed the Sea Sweeper "killed upward of four thousand fish per day." Sustain sales dipped, but outrage is short-lived these days, and now the company is doing better than ever.

Standing on the repurposed oil derrick, Vince observes the Great Pacific Garbage Patch. It doesn't look how he expected. Sure, there are undulating blobs of gray sludge, but there are also large swaths that don't appear to have any trash at all. Some of it can't be seen by the human eye—an invisible broth of microplastics hugging the surface. The only real clue it's there is the cloudiness, hardly the tropical blue you'd see on an Instagram travel blog. The refreshing sea salt smell one might expect from the tropics is also absent, tainted with an odor more like sauerkraut.

Walsh's right-hand man, Alan Shaw, interrupts Vince with a bear paw-sized clap on the back. The man looks like he was born for sea living—bearded and muscled and sunburnt, with ancient, salt-crusted work boots and a sweaty red bandana tied around his head. The only part of him that seems at odds with the seafaring life is his smile—toothpaste-commercial white. No scurvy here. Vince smiles back but doesn't show his teeth.

"Welcome to the future," Shaw says, his voice echoing across the derrick. "Another man's trash, right?"

Vince nods, not sure how to respond.

"The Patch," Shaw continues, looking out past the guard rail. "She's generous, all right."

"She?" Vince asks, cocking an eyebrow and lifting his notepad.

Shaw laughs, looks away, goes even redder than his sunburn. "Well, huh . . . how do I explain it? Pagans worship plants and animals, give thanks for what they provide. We, uh, well . . ."

Shaw stares at his feet, shaking his head. It's odd seeing a big burly guy like him do that, but Vince gives him an out.

"I get it," Vince says. "Gives you a job and someone else a shirt. All hail the Patch."

"All hail, indeed," he says, staring past the horizon line of bobbing trash, gritting his teeth.

They linger for a second, saying nothing before Shaw dismisses himself to prep a newly filled storage crate.

But Vince doesn't have long on his own before Walsh returns from her supervision duties. She invites Vince to lunch inside the derrick, where the crew eats every meal together. The full-time chef has whipped up a mean clam chowder—the clams caught and transported from elsewhere of course, plastic-free to the degree possible. Vince grabs a bowl and sits at the long metal table bolted to the floor. The crew of ten trickles in behind, two of them sitting on either side of Vince.

"You ever worked a job like this?" one of them asks, chowder straining through his beard, though he doesn't seem to notice. "Real physical work, exhausting, dangerous."

"Dangerous?" Vince asks, setting down his spoon and fumbling once more for his notepad.

"Hey, stop grilling the man," the worker on Vince's other side says—one of only two women in the room.

"No, I don't mind," Vince says. "I did landscaping for a summer, ran over my foot with a mower once. There's a chunk missing from my—well, never mind, that's not good lunch conversation. What makes this job dangerous?"

His notepad is on full display now.

The man wipes his beard clean with the back of his hand and glances behind Vince. Vince turns just in time to see a silent conversation of looks between the man and Walsh. Walsh squints, an icy expression that melts away as soon as she sees Vince watching. She turns away, snatching a handful of oyster crackers for her chowder but keeping her ear cocked toward the worker.

"Hey, uh . . ." the man says, the 'uh' trailing on like a slowly downloading thought. "You follow NFL? We don't get internet out here. Haven't heard how the Patriots are doing."

That electric feel Vince got at the mention of "danger" dissipates with the subject change, but this could still be an opportunity. Vince does in fact know how the Patriots are doing—leverage.

"Sure," he says, grinning. "You gonna answer my question first?"

The man opens his mouth, says nothing, and looks down at a digital watch that's clearly waterlogged and broken. He stands up and grabs his half-eaten bowl of chowder.

"Listen," he says. "I'd love to talk, but I—"

The whole derrick convulses. Metal plates smash into the wall. The woman next to Vince flies into the side of the table stomach-first, gets the wind knocked out of her. The remaining chowder in Vince's bowl douses his pants and the chowder in his gut comes up with the sudden movement, soaking his shirt. Everyone's yelling. Everyone except Walsh and Shaw—they're conversing without words. Walsh nods at Shaw, who shakes his head no. When Walsh widens her eyes at him and refuses to blink, Shaw slams his hand down on the table, metal silverware clattering, and storms out of the room. The derrick reaches equilibrium once more, the sea calming beneath them.

"What was that?" Vince asks Walsh, his hands dripping in thick, fishy broth.

"Rogue wave," Walsh responds too quickly. "Happens all the time. How about you get cleaned up and then we'll continue our interview?"

Before Vince can respond, Walsh leaves the room, maneuvering around her workers as they kneel to clean up the mess. Her stride is smooth, calm—nothing like Shaw's when he left. Vince wonders what they were fighting about.

He climbs the metal stairs to the bedroom they gave him, where his last set of clean clothes is. He isn't exactly sure how the claustrophobic shower here works, so he does his best wiping himself off at the sink.

But just as he's about to pull off his ruined shirt, he notices something outside the porthole window. The Patch is farther back, practically on the horizon. Not only that—it looks like it's speeding away, lightning fast. Vince checks his footing to see if a wave is pulling the derrick away from the Patch, but no, there's no feeling of movement save for the slight bob of the ocean. When he looks downward through the window, the water is as still as it would be on a windless day. He squints at the Patch again—it's even farther now. Questions bubble to the surface—dozens of them. Plenty unfit for this *Forbes* article, but hey, he's got time—why not chase his curiosity?

Vince finishes getting changed, then heads to the exterior part of the derrick. A salty mist blows up from the ocean and stings his eyes, but when his vision clears, he sees Walsh alone at the edge of the walkway. The mist obscures her, cloaks the vibrancy of her red hair and her emerald shirt, but Vince can tell her head is bowed and hands are folded together. A prayer? She never mentioned growing up religious. He approaches, and as he gets closer he can hear her saying something. No headset on—she's talking to herself. Or to someone. But before Vince can make out any of the words, she lifts her head and turns to greet him, her movement slow and deliberate. Vince's ears grow hot. He says the first thing that comes to mind.

"Does the Patch normally move like that?"

"Currents," Walsh says, nodding and narrowing her eyes.

"Pretty fast currents," Vince says, noticing that the Patch is no longer visible—fallen off the edge of the world. "Has anyone ever gotten injured on the job?"

"I thought '30 Under 30' was supposed to be a celebratory series." Walsh grins, then tucks a necklace into her shirt. Vince hadn't seen it before—there's an ornament on it. A gray plastic shard. Not the kind of jewelry he'd expect a CEO to wear.

"It is," Vince says. "I'm not writing a hit piece. Just wanting to understand the whole picture—"

"How about we save your questions for another time?"
Walsh says before wandering off.

So much for answers. Maybe if there were booze
onboard it'd be easier to get Walsh, Shaw, or anyone else
here to spill the company's dirt. Probably not an approved
interview technique in the Big Book of Journalistic Ethics,
but . . .

Vince wipes his forehead, a slick of sweat coating his
palm. The tops of his hands are red too. He forgot to pack
sunscreen, and the itch is already setting in. He'll lie down
for a couple hours and provide time for things to cool off and
workers to finish their shifts. The interviews—interroga-
tions?—can wait. Time to brainstorm a new tactic.

———

NO ONE SPEAKS to Vince at dinner. Not when he asks
about the company, about the Patch, or even about the Patriots. Not a word. But they're not talking to each other, either;
just briefly held glances before their eyes return to their
chicken kebabs. Maybe this is part of the company culture—
talkative lunches and silent dinners. Or the workers could
just be tired from a full day of lifting heavy equipment and
baking in the sun. Still, Vince fidgets in his seat, wondering if
the atmosphere would be different if he were out of the
room. He tries to eat fast. There's enough info for the article
in his notebook—nothing groundbreaking, but serviceable at
least. To hell with pulling teeth for . . . what? A juicy tidbit
about the Patch, or workplace hazards that won't make it
into the article anyway?

Vince is bringing his metal plate over to the sink when
Shaw claps a hand on his shoulder. Vince jumps and almost
spills his plate.

"Didn't mean to scare you, bud," Shaw says, his eyes

glazed over. "Just wanted to pour a drink for our guest of honor."

He smiles, barely, whiskered lips twitching upward before falling flat. He's holding a bottle of whiskey. Vince typically doesn't drink, but the man looks like he needs one, and it'd be a pity to make him drink alone.

"Sure," Vince says, setting down his plate. "Thanks."

Shaw pinches two cloudy glasses between his fingers and pours a couple fingers of whiskey each. Vince takes one and raises his glass.

"Cheers," he says. Glasses clinking is the only sound in the room.

The whiskey has a strange burn, more cool than warm. Tastes a little like paint thinner, but Vince shouldn't expect the good stuff when the closest liquor store is hundreds of miles away.

Shaw goes to drink as well, but he pauses before raising it to his lips. The worker behind him—the man who spoke to Vince at lunch—gets up from his seat, glances at Shaw ever so briefly, and then backs into him. The full glass tumbles from Shaw's hand and smashes against the floor. Everyone stands, but not in a sudden sort of way. They get up gradually, each abandoning their meals and staring at the floor.

"S-sorry," the clumsy worker says, but he's looking at Vince when he says it.

Vince furrows his eyebrows, the last of the whiskey sliding down his throat. He takes a moment to taste it. Not just cheap—there's something off about it.

Shaw doesn't bother to clean up the glass. His whole face twitches as he stumbles out of the room, moving like a drunk man even though he's sober. The other man follows, and the rest of the workers stay. They're looking at Vince now, peeking up once every few seconds as if they're actors in a play and Vince has forgotten his line. The air in the room is thick, stagnant—above sea level, but under the sea.

It's time to leave. Vince skirts around the broken glass, nods a quick thank you to the crew, and bolts the second he's through the door. Fresh air is what he needs, and he sucks it in greedily once he's on the exterior walkway. It's dusk now, the sky bloody with colors spilling out of the sun and into the clouds.

And the Patch. It's closer. Much closer than it was this morning. Higher up too. A growth spurt?

Vince blinks several times, checking to make sure the heat hasn't gotten to him. A wave of fatigue hits—sudden, severe. It's as if his sleeping cabin one level up is too far away to reach and the walkway is a fine place for a nap. It'd be ludicrous to sleep in the middle of a work site, but he finds himself sitting down. Even from this position, the dizziness washes over him, and it feels like the time his eardrum burst —unshakable vertigo and a wind tunnel howling through his skull. He presses his palms to his ears. This isn't right. He lies down. Not right at all. And just before he passes out, he sees the Patch swell to greet him.

———

THE STENCH of salty rot fills Vince's nose, and each breath feels like water squeezing into his lungs. His eyes blink open, blurry at first, partly from an unexplained head wound and partly from the constant motion—not the typical undulations of the sea. No, he's being thrashed about, high above sea level, flying with the gulls but somehow anchored to the ocean. By what? He looks down and gradually his eyes clear.

It's clutching him—the Patch; a fist of fishing nets, plastic sludge, and corporate logos slicked gray with algae. Vince shakes his head to clear a hole for his mouth, and dislodged trash plunges hundreds of feet, rejoining the Patch below. Still, breathing doesn't come easy. The Patch squeezes his ribs, moments away from cracking them. Vince sucks in air as if through a cocktail straw.

Below is the derrick—so much smaller from up here—and dotting the platforms are the workers. They gaze upward in— what? Wonder? Terror? Admiration? Vince can't make out their expressions. A swaying woman with red hair—Walsh, most likely—is yelling. Her shouts leap between octaves, raw and ragged, but her words are lost among the whistling wind and crying gulls. Her arms are raised in worship or surrender, and her feet struggle to keep their balance. The shouting lasts another few minutes, the Patch digging into Vince's ribs all the while, twitching with eagerness. Vince grunts and writhes, but his bonds only tighten.

When Walsh's speech—prayer, incantation?—ends, a unified chant comes from the entire crew, words flowing automatically like Catholics delivering their "and also with you." The words become mush by the time they reach the cloud bank, but from their tone, Vince senses more remorse than resolution.

Without warning, he's tugged upward at a great speed, and he's briefly grateful for the Patch's firm hold—to fall from here would be instant death. But to rise ever higher in this monster's possession? Not much more promising. Vince's head bends back, eyes feeling like they'll bust out the back of his skull. There's no way of knowing how high up he is now. He can no longer move his head to see the crew, the congregants. Even if he could, the clouds would block his view. He's totally alone now. No witnesses for what's about to happen. Piss runs down his leg and falls like rain. He wishes he believed in a god to pray to—perhaps he's just met Her.

And just as abruptly as the Patch ascended, it halts,

whiplashing Vince's rag-doll body. A muscle in his neck tears. A vertebra pops. He bites off his tongue, and it tumbles into the sea. His screams are no longer impeded by excess flesh. And as gradually as a pot boiling with frogs inside, the fishing nets tighten around Vince, cutting into his skin. Blood blooms in diamond patterns, dripping down through the clouds.

There's no breath left inside Vince, no energy for resistance. He witnesses, from the outside, his body being crushed. He's dissociating, looking on like a sympathetic stranger. And he thanks the universe that there is an end to all things.

THE LORD ABOVE

Coated in blood and roach bits, I pounded on Eli's door, begging that cheating piece of shit for a place to stay. I even begged him to sleep in the same bed with me, to hold me like he used to, to plug in a night light—a fucking *night light*. But believe me, I wouldn't have done it were it not for my landlord situation.

Following our breakup—well, our *third* breakup—I called it quits for good. No more "maybe things'll cool down in a couple days" or "maybe I really *can* fix him." I'd done far too much of that, and my friends made sure to tell me. Even though our home had two stories, anything short of a football stadium wouldn't have been big enough for the both of us. I would've loved to keep the place for myself, but I couldn't afford it, and no one I knew was looking for a roommate. Eli, on the other hand, had a roommate lined up already: Some burly dude he'd been seeing for months behind my back—and once, in *front* of my back while I experienced a bout of sleep paralysis, witnessing everything but unable to move or shout. When Eli came to me saying what's-his-name had been added to the lease, I about smacked him in the jaw.

Next day, the movers were there, or the moving truck, anyway. I couldn't afford to hire anyone to lug my shit around. In the process of loading the truck myself, I dropped a bookshelf down the stairs and smashed it to bits, snapped the leg off a chair when it caught on the door frame, and tweaked my back lifting—of all things—my acoustic guitar case. Not having a new place just yet, I slept in the moving truck that night, and believe you me, sleeping upright in one of those seats destroys your goddamn back.

It was a relief, then, when the third studio apartment I toured was ready for me that very day. The place was nothing special: musty smell, leaky fridge, landlord living right upstairs. But I didn't need special. I needed something that wasn't a fucking U-Haul—a fully horizontal night's rest in a double bed. Even without knowing what I know now, I was stupid to sign a lease in the first place. The property manager was the oldest tweaker I'd ever seen, wrinkled like a sphinx cat, every gray fold of skin pocked with track marks. She never made eye contact with me for more than a few seconds, instead staring intently at the ceiling. I followed her eyes to see if there was some water damage or mold I needed to be concerned about, but I didn't see anything—just the bare wooden boards of the upstairs unit. A little odd, for sure—no paneling or popcorn ceiling—but not something that would otherwise draw my attention.

As I signed the lease, however, two clauses caught my eye, and they were strange enough that I hesitated, with my pen hovering over the page: "Section 2A: Tenant agrees to grant Landlord unrestricted access to the unit at any time," and "Section 4C: Tenant agrees to notify Landlord of absences from unit longer than 48 hours." I wasn't sure either clause would hold up in a court of law, but fighting to change the lease sounded exhausting. All I wanted was a place to rest, free of cheaters and their hot young arm candy. So, I signed.

"Wonderful, Mr. Blake," the property manager said, grinning as her eyes once more drifted to the ceiling.

Her fingers trembled as she drew the key from her pocket and gave it to me, cupping my hand in her clammy palm. I grabbed the key, reminding myself to wash my hands ASAP, and took out my checkbook. I didn't quite have enough to pay that day, but the banks closed in ten minutes and my direct-deposit paycheck would come in tomorrow. It'd work out fine. I handed the woman the check.

"Thank you very much." She folded the check down the middle several times and pinched it into a sharp crease. "The lord is upstairs should you need anything."

"Excuse me?" I asked, not sure I'd heard her right.

She pointed to the ceiling, her fingernail like a cheese-yellow letter opener.

"For maintenance requests and the like," she added. "It's in the lease, my dear."

My questions unanswered but my desire for conversation deteriorating, I nodded and saw the woman out. She got into her rusted-out Lincoln and screeched away, nearly clipping my U-Haul in her rush to get who-knows-where—probably a bridge club or a drug deal.

I got to work unloading the truck one box and piece of furniture at a time. One shelf I dragged across the wood floor, leaving some nasty scratches, but to hell with my deposit. I left my first-ever apartment out of college in immaculate shape when I moved, and the landlord still dinged me for every bullshit "fix" he had to make. I'd since stopped caring about keeping my rentals in tip-top shape; I'd get financially fucked regardless.

When the sun started going down, my whole body was

sticky with sweat and my wrists bore deep purple indentations from all the heavy boxes I'd carried in. There was only my bed left, but I felt my strength waning. It was like how my body reacted when I took an extended break from the gym and returned weeks later—every muscle fiber feeling torn, bruised, and beaten, aged up sixty years.

Just as I considered saying fuck it and sleeping on the floor, someone pulled up behind the U-Haul. A white woman got out of the car, untying a server's apron and tossing it onto the car seat before locking up. She eyed me, and I must have looked an extra dose of done because she smiled.

"Need help?" she asked, then pointed her thumb toward the apartment complex, a brick cube against the fading dusk. "You're moving in, right?"

"Yes and yes," I said. "But it looks like you just got off work. I can probably—"

"Nah, it's good," she said. "I'm strong."

She winked at me, and for a moment I wondered if she was flirting. I'd wait to tell her I was gay until after we got the bed inside.

Two minutes later, we had the mattress through the door and dumped that bad boy on the floor. My neighbor hustled back to the U-Haul for the box spring, and I ambled after her, my calf muscles burning every step of the way. Once we got the last of it inside, she raised her hand over the un-feng shui-ed mess of a room. We high-fived.

"Jasmine," she said. "I'm right across the hall, in number two."

"Sean," I replied. "Thanks so much. I'd offer you a beer, but—"

"No way, neighbor, I'm offering you one. Want to see my place?"

I scratched the back of my neck, trying to read her signals. Women had hit on me before, but I always learned about it later from Eli, who called me "the chick magnet who wished he was a dick magnet." It was a shitty thing to say, transphobic even, but hey, I was done with him and under no obligation to police his behavior. Even if Jasmine *was* hitting on me, I was lonely. I'd lived with plenty of roommates throughout the years, but never alone in a dingy studio.

"Sure," I said. "You . . . you should probably know I'm gay."

"Oh, I know," she said. "Or I figured, anyway."

My voice wasn't particularly femme, but she probably saw something in my boxes: the pride flag I'd hung up at half a dozen apartments; the gender studies books I'd saved from back in college even though they made my head hurt (thanks, Judith Butler). However Jasmine figured it out didn't really matter. What mattered was that she didn't seem fazed. I felt myself relax a little. I was ready for a beer.

When we got to her door, she held out a hand for me to wait a minute while she peeked inside. I figured she probably wasn't used to company and didn't want a pile of dirty dishes or a nightstand littered with sex toys to embarrass her. Not that I'd be shocked by either—if anything, they'd be signs of a kindred spirit. After a moment of peeking around, Jasmine ushered me in.

"Sorry," she said. "Had to check for . . . well, you'll find out. This place, this building is—"

"Shitty?"

"Yeah, the buggy kind of shitty. Not bed bugs, just roaches."

"Just roaches," I repeated, half grinning, half grimacing. "That's okay, I've seen worse. When I lived in Texas, we sometimes got snakes in the basement. My dad used to chop their heads off with a shovel."

Jasmine opened the fridge, which droned a wet, electric buzz. I flashed back to my two days on the high school football team as she tossed me a can of beer. I caught it, barely, and was surprised to find that something so small felt so heavy in my hands.

"It's not a craft brew, but it's something," she said. "You can sit on the couch if you want. Sorry about the cat litter on the cushion. She likes to—"

"You have a cat too?" I said, cracking open the beer as my voice climbed an octave. "Where is she?"

"She likes to hide during the day. Not sure how she does it in this tiny apartment, but . . . well, it's weird. She seems scared to come out. Maybe it's the roaches."

"Yeah, my cat will attack anything that moves. Even me, sometimes."

I poked my head around the room until I found the two green eyes flashing under the bed. A hiss from the darkness.

"I'm picking mine up later—wanted to have my stuff moved in first," I added, trying to coax the cat out without getting bitten. "Anyway, he's still at my ex's place, and that fucker better remember to feed him. Ouch!"

A flash of ivory claws tore my arm from the shadows. I pulled away and wiped at the beads of blood.

"Shit," Jasmine said, dashing to her medicine cabinet. "Sorry. I've got some antiseptic. . . . Jesus, you should see Ginger when the landlord comes by. Goes fucking ballistic."

"Yeah, about the landlord . . ." I said, running my bleeding arm under the faucet.

Jasmine poked her head out of the tiny bathroom, letting the antiseptic soak into a cotton ball. Her eyes were wide.

"He's creepy as hell," she said. "Only saw him once. Got home late from a shift, and he was in the hall, just sorta pacing. He jumped when he saw me, like he was doing something wrong. And I was like, damn, dude, this is *your* building, you know that? He must be a night owl. Never seen him during the day, and he's never answered the door when I've knocked."

"What's he look like?"

Jasmine opened her mouth, then frowned, licked her lips. Something was bothering her.

"I don't remember," she paused, lost in her own world longer than I was comfortable with. "I'm forgetting a lot of stuff lately."

While I was eager to spend time with Jasmine, the exhaustion of the day set in for both of us. We talked about work, cats, and shitty men as we finished our beers, then Jasmine called it a night.

"I'm tired," she said. "Can't seem to get enough sleep these past few months. But hey, let's go out sometime soon. I'll show you the neighborhood. There's a great Mexican place around the block. And the worst coffee shop in the goddamn world right next to it. You'll see what I mean."

We made plans and parted ways. I walked across the hall to my apartment and turned on the lights, then promptly turned them off again when I saw, as Jasmine promised, the roaches. It was child logic; put the blanket over your head and the monsters no longer exist. But I quickly came to my senses and lit up the room once more. Most of the roaches had already scattered, no longer congregating beside my stand mixer, but a few were still skittering up the yellowing walls. Fifty of them at least, moving like a funeral procession for the kin they knew I'd be killing once I got a flip-flop in hand. But I couldn't kill them yet; I was frozen in place, transfixed. They reached the exposed ceiling and, one by one, crawled through a small opening between the floorboards above.

It was then that I noticed the squeak of the lord pacing overhead. Back and forth, and back and forth. And even when the last of the roaches slipped through the cracks into his unit, he didn't stop pacing. It was strange, especially given that he appeared to be walking past where they would emerge. Did he notice them? Did he even care? At least he was living in the filth with his tenants, not one of those mansion-on-the-hill types who avoided their own rental properties like the plague.

Then he whispered. Nothing I could decipher, but certainly words. Soft, affectionate-sounding. A single "hm" like a laugh. Who the hell was this guy? Didn't he live alone?

Creeped the hell out, I turned out the lights, made a mental note to buy some roach traps, and crawled into bed. The pacing continued for a while, as did the murmurings. On a normal night, I might have struggled to fall asleep with this going on, but my body felt like tenderized meat, and all it took was a pillow wrapped around my ears to drown out the noise. I fell into the deepest sleep I'd had in a while.

I WOKE up late the next day, sunlight beaming down on my face through the broken teeth on the blinds. My phone showed six texts and two voicemails from my boss. Shit. Today was the world premiere of the Mermaid Frappé, a blue and green cavity-carver of a drink that "Starfucks" had been hyping for the past month. There'd be cars around the block just like every other time a new novelty drink came out. And by now, with me two hours late to my shift, those cars were probably wrapped around the block a second time, half of them honking, drivers screaming profanities, and everyone finding out, after a long-ass wait, that the drink wasn't even that good.

Of course, my boss fired me. Can't say I was surprised, but the fact that today would be my last paycheck (eaten up almost entirely by rent and the deposit) didn't set well with my stomach. I wasn't looking forward to the nasty conversation that would come the first of next month when I didn't have a dollar to my name. Hopefully a job would come before then, but my boss would be a terrible reference when potential employers called him—"Sean? What can I say? Late all the time, always confuses oat milk with almond milk, doesn't abide by the corporate-approved music playlist. He's a mess!"

Well, mess that I was, I decided to save the job search for tomorrow. There was already one unpleasant task ahead of me today—a visit to Eli's to pick up my cat, Snoot. A cloud hung over me as I dug my toaster out of its box, plugged it in, and made some breakfast. I put on my "broody tunes" playlist and spaced out until the smell of ash wafted toward me. Great. The toast was burnt to shit, but given my money situation, I wasn't about to toss food in the trash. Instead, I lifted the toast to my lips, taste-testing the charcoal bottom.

That was when something dripped from the ceiling and landed on my breakfast. Miniscule droplets of the liquid ricocheted onto my tongue. I dropped the toast on the floor and spat into the sink. Whatever it was tasted salty. I put my mouth under the faucet and let it run for a minute, gargling away whatever the hell that substance had been. Only after I was sure I'd eradicated it did I check the toast on the floor. The liquid had already soaked into the bread, and even among the expanse of crusty black craters, a patch of wet was visible. I sighed and, ignoring my frugal instincts, tossed the toast in a plastic trash bag. I'd find something else to eat right after I discovered what was dripping from the landlord's room. The ring on the ceiling was purple, and I wondered if it might've come from a spilled bottle of wine.

In any case, it was time to introduce myself to the man —"Hi, I'm the whiny, newly unemployed tenant downstairs here with my first maintenance request of many." I shuddered to think how he might respond, but there was only one way to find out.

Throwing on some proper clothes—that is, yesterday's T-shirt and some sweatpants—I opened the door to the hallway, prepared to venture upstairs. I was stopped, however, by the property manager, looking even more ancient than yesterday as she directed the movers cleaning out unit two across the hall. I peeked over but didn't see Jasmine. Damn. She'd told me just last night she'd show me around the neighborhood. Why hadn't she mentioned she was moving?

"What's going on?" I asked.

"I suggested taking it all to Goodwill," the property manager said as the movers carried out a couch. "But the tenant suggested the dump. Lord knows why."

"Sorry, what? Jasmine's leaving? All her stuff—she's just . . ."

"She broke her lease, dear. Very unexpected. As for her personal effects, maybe she's downsizing."

"From a studio apartment? No, no, it . . . I don't understand. She seemed so—"

"If you'll excuse me, dear, I need to help the movers," she said, then yelled at them in a voice like rust. "Don't bang up the wall! You'll wake the lord."

There it was again. What was it with the "lord" business? And with Jasmine leaving? The news put me in a dark place, the kind of place that might've kept me nursing a bottle all day, immobile in bed, watching shitty reality TV 'til the sun came up.

But there was still much to do. I couldn't let this leak wait, nor could I leave my cat with that cheating piece of shit an hour longer. I trudged up the brown carpeted stairs. If I hadn't looked more closely, I might have missed the fact that the carpet was actually gray underneath. The brown came from the roaches, thousands of their corpses pressed into the fibers like flowers pressed into a scrapbook. I nearly threw up, but without the toast in me, there was nothing but acid stewing in my gut. Hand to my mouth just in case, I made it to the top of the stairs, keeping my eyes on the chipped blue walls with the knowledge that this building's floors and ceilings were both grotesque.

Then, the lord's door was in front of me, gray and barely tall enough for someone to walk through. I hesitated, listening before I knocked. On the other side was a sound like oil frying, crackles and hisses and bubbles, but I didn't smell any food. Something smelled earthy. I couldn't quite make out what it was. I knocked. The frying sound stopped but no one answered. I waited. Two minutes and two rounds of knocking later, still nothing. This was ridiculous. The building manager indicated the 'lord' was here—sleeping maybe, but it was noon now and not an unreasonable time for someone to pay a visit.

I looked back down the roach-crusted stairs, gagged once more, and thought about leaving and never coming back. Then I noticed the chalkboard beside the door, a pinky nail-sized piece of chalk resting on the wooden base. I guess this was where I'd leave my message, scribbling away like a teacher in a one-room schoolhouse. Not wanting to come back up here again to explain my financial situation, I decided to take care of both issues in one go: "Hi—Sean in unit #1. Leak in my ceiling—can you fix it? Also, in between jobs—might need a rent extension next month. Sorry."

I tried to set the chalk back where I'd found it, but I dropped it when a roach skittered across the board. I just left the chalk in the carpet and hustled downstairs. It was time to get my cat and some fresh air.

———

Snoot sniffed around the new, smaller living space, and while his tree wasn't set up yet, he seemed perfectly content to perch atop my stacks of boxes. I removed him only when the box of plates started wobbling. I wasn't about to deal with a floor covered in both roaches and ceramic shards.

Most of the day, we lounged together in bed, me scritching his ears with one hand while holding a book in the other—a mystery, fun and just dumb enough that I was able to piece together a few of the clues. Despite everything that preceded this moment, I felt at peace. No work to worry about. No cheating boyfriends. And really, not even unpacking. Given the roaches and strangeness of the place, I'd already given thought to breaking my lease whenever I could afford to and moving elsewhere. The boxes could stay packed until then.

What unnerved me was the silence. There was a small range of sound around which I could focus—too loud and I'd be distracted, too quiet and I'd be anxious. The latter proved to be the case as I never once heard footsteps upstairs or anyone open a door in the hallway. Was I the only tenant left? Or was it just that the other tenants were at work and, newly unemployed, I had no idea what the mid-afternoon lull sounded like?

The quiet soon got to me. I leashed up Snoot—yes, I'm that kind of cat owner—and headed around the block for some Mexican food. The place Jasmine mentioned was a little hole in the wall with neon-painted windows advertising their "world famous" tamales. I tied Snoot to the fire hydrant and popped inside to see if the restaurant's tamales deserved the title. Ten minutes later, with a clamshell container of tamales in hand, I walked back to the apartment with Snoot. I didn't want to go inside yet, so I ate my meal on the crumbling stoop, surrounded by cigarette butts but at least not roaches.

The "world famous" claim wasn't a lie. Brimming with the best thing I'd eaten in months, I held a hand to my stomach and let out a deep exhale. Snoot was lying on his back, batting at a dandelion growing through the cracks in the brick. It was cute, but damn if I didn't need to lie down and let myself digest. Sure, it had been a day of mostly nothing, but it felt even more exhausting than yesterday, chipping away at me bit by wounding bit.

"Come on, Snoot," I said, scratching his belly. "Let's go inside."

The sun was just starting to go down, and while I normally would have stayed up a few hours longer, I was ready for bed—a twelve-hour depression nap slash food coma.

Inside, I collapsed onto the bed, and Snoot climbed his perch, eyeing the ceiling. I followed his gaze, and from the looks of it, there were no more leaks—one sliver of relief to ease me into sleep. But Snoot was preoccupied. It was as if he were watching a bird up above, his claws extending and his paws kneading left, right, left, right. Restless.

Then it caught my eye—something moving between the ceiling's floorboards. I thought it might be a roach at first, but it was white and thin and angular. It grew bigger each second, and when it emerged halfway, I knew what it was—a sheet of paper from the landlord upstairs. It slipped between the boards and floated gently to the floor. I held my breath and stared for what felt like ages. Eventually, though, I had to pee—might as well get up and take a look. I inched over to that spot on the floor where, in all likelihood, a thousand roaches had fed, fucked, and died. I picked the paper up like one might pick up a sheath of snake skin.

It read, "Leak fixed. And don't worry about the money—there are other ways to pay."

In retrospect, I should have left the apartment that very

moment and slept in my car with Snoot in the passenger seat. But it was still early in the month, and whatever "other ways to pay" implied, I had time to scrape together some cash to avoid such an arrangement.

Nonetheless, I stood paralyzed, reading the note over and over again, reliving the sound of it slipping through the floorboards above. Eventually, I noticed Snoot still looking at the ceiling, licking his whiskers. I wondered if he heard something I didn't—the first rustles of another note slithering down to me. But when he hissed at nothing whatsoever, I lunged toward him and scooped him into my arms, then jumped into bed. Whether I was his protector or he was mine, I wasn't sure, but it felt better having him with me. Even though the sun was barely down, it was time for bed—remain conscious any longer and I might have come unglued.

The door. I had to make sure it was locked. There was only the deadbolt—the chain lock had been removed or broken—but it would have to do. I got out of bed, then double, triple, quadruple checked that the door wasn't budging. It seemed solid enough, and if anyone found a way through it, the hinges were still squeaky. I just hoped I was a light enough sleeper to hear them before anyone came in. Just in case, I took out my baseball bat and placed it beside my bed. Only once had I needed to use it—on a drunk homophobe who lived across the hall from me in the college dorms, but boy I grateful to have it then. The asshole never bothered me again.

It took longer than the previous night to fall asleep. Snoot seemed restless, too, but that might've just been from the move. He paced around the bed for a while, sometimes in circles, his claws puncturing the sheets with tiny, dry pops as they pulled away. I dragged him toward me so he'd stop, and though he gnawed at my arm, his bites soon became love nibbles. I must have fallen asleep around the time he stopped.

It was when he howled that I awoke. Well, didn't wake up entirely. My eyes were open, but my body couldn't move, as if I'd woken up while on anesthesia. The howls didn't come from beside me. Snoot had moved—or perhaps *been moved*—to the door. His silhouette meshed with another's—a human shape, none of the details discernible. Snoot was dangling from his pinched scruff, paws thrashing like he'd been thrown in a full bathtub, desperate to escape. Whoever held him did so with their thumb and forefinger, as if Snoot were a piece of trash about to be discarded. How this person could lift him up with just two fingers, I had no idea; Snoot was not a slim cat.

My lungs seized, breath caught in the middle of my throat. I worried, in my paralyzed state, that I might vomit and choke to death like a heroin user left lying on his back.

Without warning, the figure lifted Snoot to its mouth. The howling stopped. Snoot thrashed a time or two, his back legs twitching, but no sound escaped him. There was only the sound of sucking, like lips vacuuming a melon dry. Tears streamed down my face, and though it felt like my arm was lifting into the air, the movement was all part of what I prayed was a larger hallucination. My body was cadaverous yet violently alive, nerves torched to hell.

And then, well . . . I don't know what happened. I awoke late the next morning, feeling as if I'd had no sleep at all. I wasn't on the bed, but rather curled up on the kitchen floor, the corner of my blanket soaked in the fridge's leakage. Something smelled like cat piss. And big surprise, there was a puddle of the stuff by the door. I hopped around it to check the lock—still secure. But Snoot was nowhere to be seen. I checked the bathroom, under the bed, in every box—hell, even in the microwave. He was gone.

You might wonder why I didn't immediately assume what now seems obvious, but my body had long engaged in both sleep paralysis and sleepwalking. Some of the best pre-cheating memories of Eli were waking up to ask him what unconscious nonsense I'd gotten up to in the middle of the night. "Oh," he'd say, "folding everything in my underwear drawer, talking to ghosts, the usual." It wouldn't have surprised me to find that I'd hallucinated the thing feasting on my cat, then later let Snoot out into the hall while sleep-walking.

But a gut feeling nagged at me. As impossible as the terrible alternative would be, I couldn't help but entertain it. Everything about this place exuded bad vibes.

I put off the job search a little longer, instead spending the day looking for Snoot. If I couldn't find him, I'd get the fuck out of this apartment, ask my friend and now former coworker Macy if I could crash on her couch.

I checked the hallway and found nothing except for a discarded paycheck advance flyer. I knocked the other tenants' doors, but no one answered. I walked around the block calling Snoot's name. Eventually, I wound up at the coffee shop Jasmine mentioned, and desperate for something to distract me from my panic, ordered a large espresso and a cranberry scone. All the caffeine did was spike my anxiety, and as Jasmine promised, everything tasted like shit.

The search went on for another hour with no signs of Snoot. I did everything but knock on the lord's door. If any of what I saw last night was real—and if the mysterious figure was who I suspected—I wouldn't dare fuck with the man.

It seemed my only option was to call Macy after all. When I told her the heavily abridged version of my situation, she said she'd leave work at 9 p.m. and order pizza for us—of course I could stay the night. Since she was on the job, our conversation had to be brief. Hordes of people were still lining up for the Mermaid Frappé, and if she didn't hang up ASAP, the boss would fire her too. I hung up and breathed a sigh of relief.

Until nine, I did everything in my power to avoid the apartment. Sure, the lord was a night owl and probably wouldn't be up at this time doing whatever creepy shit he got up to, but being outside felt a whole hell of a lot less stressful. I popped into Walgreens, bought a light and my first pack of cigarettes in a year, and walked in a random direction. The neighborhood was still new to me, so anywhere I went held something new. I probably wouldn't live there much longer, but the area still seemed cute, roach dens aside.

I wandered for hours, smoking and stopping at the occasional bar for a drink despite my better financial judgment. The cigarettes and booze lifted my mood, though, and combined with exercise and the promise of a night in someone else's company, I was flying high by the time I got back to the apartment. Of course, Snoot was in the back of my mind the whole time, but alcohol staved off some of the pain.

It came as a surprise, then, when Snoot was waiting for me on the stoop, his orange tail flicking and his yellow eyes blinking slowly, impassively. It was dark out now, but I knew it was him; I'd never met another cat quite so fat. Only, was he skinnier than he was last night? And was his fur clumpier than usual? I'd love to say these questions mattered to me, but they didn't cross my mind then. I ran and scooped him up with tears in my eyes. Normally, he would've bitten me for doing that, but this time he remained still, the rhythm of his flicking tail unbroken. Maybe he didn't attack because he was happy to see me, and if so, the feeling was mutual as hell.

I tucked him under my arm and headed to my car. We drove to Macy's place, arriving at the same time as her. She was still wearing her green apron, and I stuck out my tongue when I saw it, following up with a smile seconds later. Macy knew what was up.

"I'll take this thing off before it gives you flashbacks," she said, untying the apron and then hugging me. "Miss you, bitch. I mean, I'm little envious you got fired, but—"

"It's not as liberating as I thought it would be," I said. "Thanks for doing this."

"No problem. So you got a cheating boyfriend and a bug problem?"

"Among other things." For a second I thought about going into specifics, but she might've thought I was crazy. "Anyway, let's eat pizza and watch a fucking movie. You cool if Snoot comes in?"

Macy bent down to pet my cat, her words morphing into a baby voice, "As long as he doesn't piss on the carpet, okay, bb?"

"He's good at avoiding that," then, thinking of the mess this morning, " . . . mostly."

The night was a blast. We curled up on the couch, our fingers greasy and our eyes wet as we commiserated over our breakups. I didn't know Macy had broken up with Jess, but apparently it happened over text during her lunch break just yesterday. With me being gone—well, fired—she had to work a double shift, holding back tears the whole time. I felt bad, but she assured me it wasn't my fault and changed the subject to Eli. Even though we had some zombie movie on in the background, it was our conversation that I most remember from that night. Bonding through shared pain, making jokes at our exes' expense, and retroactively justifying why the relationships had been a mistake from the start.

Around 2 a.m., we said goodnight. Macy shuffled to her bedroom and closed the door. I laid down on the couch, my feet protruding off the other end a few inches and my neck smashed against the armrest at a severe angle. But it was more comfortable than my apartment, at least psychologically.

Snoot hopped up to the windowsill and stared out at the street. He normally came to bed with me, but this was the third place he'd stayed at in under a week; I could excuse the atypical behavior. Part of me also liked him there, at attention, gazing out at the bar crawlers stumbling home and racers screeching down the road when no cops were in sight. Snoot was my guardian, and under his watch, I slept well.

At least until the tapping started—a fingernail against the window. My eyes opened, and this time, I could move but didn't dare. Someone was in the bush; I couldn't make out their features. Snoot was looking at them, licking the glass where the stranger's face pressed in. A louder knock, and this time I jumped a little, glanced around the room for a light switch. It was closer to the window than I felt comfortable with. I thought about turning on my phone flashlight, but when I took it out, the battery was dead. Fuck.

Tap. Taptap.

"Macy," I called, but my voice caught in my throat, as if I were having an allergic reaction.

When the stranger spoke, his words came out both silken and raspy. How he could sound both those ways at once, I had no idea.

"Let me in," he said. "You have what's mine."

I sat up straighter and pressed my ass as far back into the couch's armrest as I could, the wooden frame groaning against me. My heart felt like it was pumping sludge.

"Fuck off," I said, finding my voice. "I'll call the—I'll call the police."

Of course, I didn't really want to do that. What would the

cops do? Pull up too late? Call me crazy? Chastise me for wasting their time?

"Don't," the stranger said, the bushes rustling around him. "You'll make it worse for yourself."

"Macy!" I said, turning toward her bedroom door. "Macy, help!"

But when I looked back at the window, the stranger was gone. Snoot sat there, curled up and purring.

When Macy's door opened, she came out in red flannel pajama pants and an oversized Rage Against the Machine T-shirt. She threw on the light switch, squinting at me.

"What's going on?" she asked.

"There's . . . there was someone out there, knocking on the window."

"What?"

"Yeah, he wanted to be let in."

"You sure it wasn't just some drunk dude? There are three bars on this block alone."

I paused, mouth agape, wanting to go into all the reasons I thought otherwise, but all I'd told Macy about was the roaches. The rest was just paranoia. At least, I hoped so.

"Listen," she said. "That's just what goes down in this neighborhood. If you yell at them, they go away. Looks like he's gone already. Anyway, I really should get some sleep. I have work at seven."

"Okay," I said, heat spreading across my neck. "Sorry, Macy."

"It's all good. See you in the morning."

The rest of the night was uneventful, but I didn't sleep a wink.

———

IN THE MORNING, Snoot was once again nowhere to be found. How I'd missed him leaving his spot by the window, I'm not sure. Maybe I glazed over for a moment, not asleep but not awake either. Regardless, I was still searching for him by the time Macy donned her green apron for work.

"He's probably under a piece of furniture or something," she said, checking her phone for the time. "Hey, make sure to lock up when you go, okay? And good luck with the job search. Let me know if you need to stay another night."

"Thanks, Mace," I said, eyeing my surroundings for hiding spots I'd missed.

Macy left. Sighing, I shuffled over to the window and gazed out at the yard, a week overdue for mowing. Something caught my eye on the other side of the windowsill—something crawling, writhing. Roaches. Dozens of them.

"Fuck!" I said and checked the window's lock and weather seal to make sure none could slip in.

I took a moment to talk myself down from a dangerous conclusion. Roaches lived everywhere, right? They hadn't followed me from the apartment, riding on the hunched back of whoever had—no, no, that was ridiculous. Best to keep it out of mind.

An almost inaudible sound like fabric rubbing against fabric came from somewhere in the room. I whipped around and cocked my ear to find it. Ah, under the armchair—the leather one with all the food crumbs. I got down on my knees and peeked to look under it. Sure enough, there were two glowing yellow eyes, Snoot snug in his new hidey-hole. I'd have to rip him out, hissing and claws clinging to the carpet the whole way. But I'd done it before.

The space between the springy bottom and the floor was narrow, and my arm almost didn't fit, but as soon as I wedged it in, Snoot started scratching. Not playful scratches, but scratches guaranteed to leave streaks of blood under the chair. I gritted my teeth and grabbed more aggressively, my hand snatching Snoot's scruff on the fourth swing. By then, my forearm throbbed, hot and leaking. I dragged Snoot out, inch by inch, fighting the whole way, and as he got closer to the world outside his den, smoke began to rise. It was almost indiscernible at first, like a lit candle's gray, wavering column. But as soon as Snoot's head reached the outside, bathed in a morning sunbeam, he burst into flames, cat hair curling into liquid black shrivels. There was a shrieking like I'd never heard before, the kind normally reserved for rabbits killed by cats, not cats killed by . . . what, exactly? I let go. I screamed. But it was unstoppable now, the flames licking the chair's leather, spreading across the dry carpet as if it were a prairie in a drought, the whoosh of an inferno finding its spark. The sound of a cat in agony petered out. Half the living room was engulfed. There was nothing I could do.

I ran out the front door, hopped into my car, and sped away like a street racer, peeling through a red light, around some pedestrians using the crosswalk. I could already see smoke rising in my rearview. What the fuck was happening?

Before I knew it, I was back at the apartment, back to the landlord, likely still asleep with his black curtains drawn and the sun overhead. Terror flowed through me, but also a rage yet unquenched. It was him. It had to be him. What had he done to make Snoot burn? I sprinted from the car, not bothering to slam the door shut. I smashed through the apartment's entrance shoulder-first, pane of glass cracking and arm bruising, but I was in. Upstairs. That's where I'd go. March right up those nasty-ass steps and do the same damn thing—smash my way in, break my fucking collarbone if I had to. Not taking appointments during the daytime? Too damn bad. I wasn't about to leave another chalkboard message; it would be a face-to-face confrontation or nothing. There was the door, gray and small, hopefully as brittle as it looked. I backed up several steps, my feet crunching on you-know-what. I charged. The fucking door broke at the lock. Something broke inside me, too—a sharp internal pinch that didn't let up. It didn't matter. I was in.

But as the door swung open, a tide unleashed. The dam burst, millions of roaches swarming my flesh, fluttering in my ear with their wax paper wings, honing in on whatever warm crevice my body had to offer. I gasped and sucked some into my windpipe. I coughed and fewer came out than in.

There was no choice but to run in the opposite direction. Which direction that was, I couldn't tell. I could see nothing through the cloud—nothing save for the skittering, fluttering carapaces churning like a tornado around me. I reached for the handrail, and on the third try, found it. Like a half-drowned man pulling himself to shore on a rope, I tugged myself down the stairs, stumbled when I couldn't see one step give way to the next, and fell headfirst onto the carpet, not soft enough to cushion my fall. Warm blood trickled down my forehead. I closed my eyes, seeing stars but at least not the plague of bugs around me. I kept going. My knee throbbed, strained in the fall. And the incessant buzzing surrounded me, growing louder each moment, tinnitus-inducing in its intensity. Worst were the roaches who'd found my ears and burrowed in, prickling my eardrums with each step.

Somehow I got to the stoop, but as much as I wanted to keep running, I had to do something first. Roaches still buzzing around inside my lungs, I coughed and took out my pack of smokes. I held the pack under my lighter and set it ablaze, then tossed it into the apartment building. The roaches caught on fire first. Then the wallpaper.

When I was certain the blaze would destroy the place, I sprinted to my car, started it up, and didn't bother to close the door before peeling out. For the second time that day, a building burned in my rearview mirror. My car door knocked against a parked truck and slammed itself shut, a red scrape gouged on its side. But I kept driving and didn't stop until I reached Eli's, the mucus-soaked corpse of a roach dripping down my steering wheel, slow as tar. The others had probably left my ears by now, but I could still feel their phantom limbs. I smacked the side of my head like a swimmer trying to expel trapped water.

As soon as the car lurched into park, I broke into sobs. The landlord paid for what he did, but it hadn't brought Snoot back. And how long would it be before the blame fell on me? Sean Parsons: cat killer, landlord murderer, and double arsonist. I'd hide out at Eli's for one night only. After that, I'd ditch town and find a new place to stay. A new place, with a new lord.

UNDER THE HOOF, UPON THE HORNS

This is Hugo's eighteenth time seeing the video. We rewatch it together every year before the run; or rather, I watch it while he sits beside me on the couch, eyes glued to a fantasy novel. I've never understood why he reads that sword-and-sorcery junk, or why he reads in general.

"Son, watch," I tell him. "Big moment's coming up— made the national highlight reel."

"I know, Dad," he says, glaring at me the way only a teenager can.

The VHS hisses, worn from years of watching and rewinding and watching again. I worry the player will eat the tape, leaving the memory to exist only in my head. But surely another recording is out there. Hugo can help me find one on the internet.

"Look," I say, leaning forward and pointing at the screen. "Here it comes—two thousand pounds of muscle. And . . . bam! Ooh, I can still feel it."

I massage my right ear—or what remains of it—between my thumb and forefinger. A bull trampled and tore off a chunk twenty years back. When I got up from the cobblestone, caught in the stampede of man and beast, I didn't have time to look for what I'd lost, probably stuck to the bull's hoof like chewing gum.

"If that hoof had been even an inch closer, I would've been gone," I tell Hugo, who sinks farther into the couch and holds the book closer to his face. "You wouldn't be alive."

He sighs and rests the book on his chest.

"Well, thanks for not dying, Dad," he says.

The TV shows me stumbling to my feet, narrowly avoiding another bull's horns as I plug the geyser of blood erupting from my head. A lesser man would've quit then, but I staggered to the finish line. All of Pamplona cheered.

"This is how I became a man," I say. "And how you'll become one too."

Hugo picks up his book again, eyes glassy as they dart across the page.

He'll come around. I'll make sure of it.

———

"YOUR GRANDFATHER GOT LUCKIER than I did," I tell Hugo as we walk toward the starting line, past tall buildings bricked red and gold. "Ran in front of a bull for a full fifteen seconds. Somehow didn't get gored, but he got the biggest applause of any runner that year. Of course, he's a bit of a storyteller, so it's possible he exaggerated. At least I've got video evidence to back *my* story up."

I wink, but Hugo isn't looking at me. He moves forward like a robot, legs operating on autopilot, arms and face locked in position.

Around us are runners outside bars, sipping—and sometimes chugging—drinks before the race begins. Maybe booze will loosen Hugo up. There are still thirty minutes until it starts, so we've got time.

"Son, let me buy you a drink," I say, dragging him toward a bar brimming with laughter and loud pop music, but nothing I recognize.

"I don't want one, Dad," Hugo says, pulling away, but I grab his arm.

"Trust me—it'll help."

Hugo orders a light beer—hardly the nerve-settling drink I had in mind, but it'll do. We sit at the bar beside two men a few years older than Hugo. Both are wearing white shirts, white pants, and red bandanas, so we know they're runners. Hugo refused to wear the same, but hell, as long as he's running, he can skirt some of the less essential traditions.

"This is my son, Hugo," I tell the men. "It's his first year running."

Hugo instantly goes red in the face and sets down his drink, pushing it back to the bartender. One of the men grabs Hugo's shoulder and goes forehead-to-forehead with him, grinning. The man's a few drinks deeper than anyone else here, and his voice cuts through the booming music easily.

"You're gonna love it, kid," he says, and when he opens his mouth, a few teeth are missing. "This is my fifth year."

His friend howls, and they clink their glasses together, spilling beer. They remind me of myself at their age—hell, even me at my current age. I grin and elbow them, tilting to show my ear wound.

"Got this at the 2000 run," I say. "Bull knocked me down and—"

But the men's attention is broken when partiers start singing "Uno de Enero"; it would hardly be the Running of the Bulls without that song. The men rush over to the group, belting the words and holding their beers above the crowd as they approach some gorgeous women. I smile and resist the urge to follow. Let them enjoy their youth.

"Can we go?" Hugo hisses through his teeth.

I hold up a finger for him to wait, chug the rest of my beer, and then wipe the foam off my mustache. We head out the door and make our way to the race.

———

I HERD Hugo to the starting line, my hand pressing against his back. When I feel his heels dig in, I regret not making him finish that beer. He's a lightweight; one would've been enough to ready him for the race.

All around us, runners are stretching, chatting, and riling up the crowd. Residents gather on their balconies, holding up colorful signs with the names of friends or family members running. Red and white festival lights zigzag from one side of the street to the other, drawing my eye to the Plaza de Toros, far off but still within squinting distance. I finger the tickets in my pocket to make sure I still have them—wouldn't want to miss the bullfights after the run, which will start any minute now.

Before joining the thousands of spectators behind the wooden barricades, I clutch Hugo's head in my hands.

"You'll be fine," I tell him. "And more importantly, when it's over you'll be a man."

As I climb to the other side, Hugo clings to the barricade like an infant to his mother's breast. I look around to see if the cameras are on him, and seeing none, exhale in relief.

"Right down the middle, son," I say, prying his hands from the wooden post. "Hugging the side is for cowards."

There are tears in his eyes, but I can only hold his hand for so long. Whatever he'll do, he'll do, and it's time I get in position farther down the route. I push through the crowd, knowing the first rocket will sound soon. Around me are drunk partiers singing off-key, tourists eating street meat, and lovers sharing a last kiss before the run. I smile, feeling electricity in the air, and I hope that Hugo feels it too.

The first rocket goes off when I'm a quarter-mile up the route, and the crowd cheers. The thunder of a thousand feet hitting the cobblestone is subtle at first but becomes almost deafening as the runners near my position. The second rocket sounds, and the bulls are released. They'll be here soon, but Hugo should arrive before them. My eyes are locked on the route, scanning one runner then the next, not wanting to miss Hugo. I'm suddenly grateful he chose not to wear the traditional running clothes; his black Queen shirt will make him easier to spot.

It's not long before I see him, and for a moment, I wish I hadn't. He's hugging the barrier, pressing his back flat against it to make himself smaller. I almost turn away, but then I notice the bull. It's massive, taller than the others by a full head, with back muscles built like mountains. It's closing in on Hugo quickly.

"C'mon, Hugo!" I shout, clapping my hands and jumping.

He whips his head in my direction, eyes wide enough to show the whites. It occurs to me that, with all the other chaos around him, he hasn't seen the bull yet.

"Hugo!" I call, and point behind him.

But it's too late. The bull scoops Hugo onto its horns and smashes through the wooden barrier, boards splitting like toothpicks. Hugo is soundless in his terror, but the onlookers behind the barrier scream and dive out of the way. In barely a second's time, the bull and Hugo are gone, disappearing down a narrow alleyway. I run in that direction, cursing under my breath and shoving people out of the way. Reaching the alley, I take a sharp turn but slip on a slick of spilled beer. Just as I hit the ground, I see the giant bull turning down an even narrower alley, its massive shoulders barely fitting through. I push myself up and, despite my newly sprained ankle, pursue the beast.

It takes only a few limping steps to realize I'm not in the best condition for a chase. I glance back to see if anyone's following, but no. It's like they've all forgotten that this boy just got carried away by an SUV-sized bull. The spectators are all back to watching the run, clapping and cheering. I think about yelling for help, but fuck that. Fuck them. I can do this myself. I take off.

Heart pounding in my chest, the adrenaline kicks in. My ankle isn't any less twisted—in fact, it's probably *more* twisted—but the throb that comes with each step is becoming easier to ignore. I soon reach the alleyway the bull went down, lined with tan limestone buildings. I hope to find the bull stuck there, horns too wide to allow passage, but it's nowhere to be seen. The alleyway is totally vacant—no people, no food carts, no pop-up tourist shops, nothing. That's strange, considering it's so close to the run; normally every crevice of Pamplona is packed with *something* during the festival.

I hobble forward—the brief pause definitely has me feeling my ankle again—and examine the ground. If Hugo was injured, a trail of blood could lead me to him, but I don't see one. Not finding blood should make me feel better, but my gut twists at the absence. I'll have to use my other senses to track them, and if a bull is one thing, it's loud, snorting and stampeding in bestial rage. But just as I see nothing, I hear nothing. It occurs to me that I don't even hear the run— no drunken whoops, no festive music, no yelps of pain from the trampled. It's dead silent. Maybe I shouldn't be surprised; it's a narrow alleyway nestled between thick rock buildings that probably don't let much sound through. But still, I only hear the patter of my own feet against the cobblestone. There's not even the distant rumble of traffic.

I speed up as the end of the narrowing alleyway approaches, and it's there that my suspicions are confirmed. The bull *was* too narrow to fit, but it forced its way through, anyway. There are two long gouges in the limestone on either side, rock ground into powder through the beast's sheer force. For a second, I hesitate to leave the claustrophobic alleyway, wondering if the bull is waiting for me just around the corner. Unfortunately, I have no choice but to accept the danger if I want to find Hugo. I peek my head out, anticipating hot, rancid breath on my cheek. Feeling none, I step out.

I find myself in a spacious plaza empty of all human life. A fountain sits at the center, dry and crusted with dead algae. A spiral of crumbling brickwork surrounds it, weeds sprouting through the cracks. A market encloses the plaza on two sides. The fruit stalls are full of moldy peaches and apples shriveled as shrunken heads, but no flies buzz around the rotting produce. Most stalls' awnings have frayed and collapsed—they'd be blowing in the wind if there were any. But just like the alleyway, the plaza is soundless.

I hesitate to call out Hugo's name, as if my voice might violate this place's pact of silence. But as soon as the thought crosses my mind, I realize it's a foolish one. After clearing my throat, I shout for my son as loud as I can. Despite my volume, my voice doesn't echo back. The sound is sucked away almost the instant it leaves my mouth. I don't shout again. If I did, I'm sure this place would be even quicker to rob me of my words. I've got its attention.

I see movement behind the market stalls. Whatever it is, it's big, but it slinks behind some wood paneling before I can get a good look. At first, I tiptoe forward until I remember that this place will devour whatever noise I make. I break into a run, closing in on the plaza and what I can only assume to be the bull.

Just as I'm about to pass the fountain, something inside catches my eye—a torn black Queen shirt. I jolt to a halt, jumping into the fountain to investigate. Did Hugo escape the bull and run away, minus his shirt? Before I can look around for Hugo, something tan, half-tucked inside the shirt, catches my attention. I unfold the fabric, and my breath catches when I discover a spongy chunk of flesh. My first thought is that it came from Hugo, but it's bloodless, the tearaway wound a white, bulbous scar. Turning it over, I discover it's an ear. And it's mine—a fact both impossible and undeniable. I bring the sliver of flesh to what remains of my right ear, and the parts fit together like puzzle pieces. There's a brief squelch and a pinch as the detached piece wriggles forward of its own accord, then my ear is whole once more. I give it a tug; the thing doesn't come off.

Before I have time to laugh or scream, my restored ear is flooded with the roar of a bull, low and thundering and not an inch away. I jump and turn, expecting to find the beast right beside me, but it's nowhere to be found. Even without a physical source, the roaring continues, and a thin, high scream seeps into the background. It's barely audible at first, but it escalates each moment until it's loud enough that I know who it belongs to. It's my scream—or the scream of my younger self. But there's nothing in my left ear; the roaring and screaming are isolated to just the one side. And when I press my palm against the right one to drown out the cacophony, it only seems to trap the sound inside.

"Stop it! Fucking stop it!" I shout.

And it does. The sound vanishes, and the restored piece of my ear sizzles for a moment before falling back off into the fountain. In seconds, it's a withered, prune-like thing and unrecognizable as part of my body.

I shudder and nearly trip as I back away. Just as I stumble out of the fountain, the massive shape I saw earlier emerges from behind the stalls. I freeze in place. It stands ten feet tall, not entirely human and not entirely bull. Its human half—or really, human *fifth*, puny compared to the rest—is wearing a black montera hat with a gaping hole through the center. Gore drips from the hole along with clumps of something gray. After the initial shock subsides, I realize it's Hugo. He's dressed head-to-toe in the clothes of a matador—shirt royal blue and embroidered with gold thread, red cape draping regally over his right side. These bright colors are what initially keep me from seeing the nightmare that is his lower half. His human legs are gone, gory stumps mounted on the horns of the bull like sausages onto pokers. Hugo's blood drips into the bull's eyes, and when the beast blinks, Hugo reaches down to wipe the liquid away. Then, the two—are they two?—approach me with a slow, powerful stride, and it takes everything in me not to cede my ground. My knees lock up, and my chest puffs out.

"Son," I say, but the word comes out as if my throat is narrow as a cocktail straw.

The bull is now close enough that I feel its breath fever-hot against my face. I'm sweating, and I have to remind my lungs to keep working—it'd be certain death if I passed out now, the bull surely itching to pummel me into the ground. But before it has a chance, Hugo speaks, monotone and stuttering more intensely than I've ever heard. Maybe that head injury crossed some wires in his brain.

"I d-d-didn't w-want to r-run," he says. "B-b-but y-you love r-running."

I open my mouth but don't know what to say. I'm not sure what he wants from me or what he's getting at.

"Listen," I say. "We'll find a way to get you—"

He says something—one syllable—but his tone is so low that I miss it.

"W-what?" I ask, and now I'm the one stuttering.

Hugo and the bull open their mouths in unison. Even though the bull roars, I know it's echoing his message—their minds linked, inseparable.

"Run!" they bellow so loudly that I stumble back into the fountain and hit my head.

But there's no time to rub away the pain. I bolt back toward the alleyway, hoping that rejoining the crowd will keep me safe. The rumble of hooves pounding against the cobblestone follows. One second they sound like they're right on my heel, and the next, they're a mile away. I'm not sure whether it's the beast varying speeds or this place toying with me, but I don't dare turn around even when the sound seems distant. My feet carry me faster than they have in twenty years, and it's clear that I've been out of the game for too long.

I turn the corner into the alleyway and, once more, feel the twist of my ankle. Only this time, there's a wet pop. Each time my heel slams into the street, fire courses through it, a burn pulsing up into my calf. The beast is right behind me, its horns once more grinding through stone walls with the ease of a knife through cake. But there's another sound too— thin metal scraping against a rough surface. I glance back only for a second, and the glint of an estoque catches my eyes. It's Hugo wielding the matador's sword, dragging it across the alley wall and showering sparks upon the ground. He isn't smiling. A lump of gray slides from his forehead to his lip only to be whisked away on a current of air, like a bug blown from the window of a speeding car. I whip my head forward and speed up, gritting my teeth as the burning coal sensation prickles through my foot.

The end of the alleyway approaches. I steel myself for the next turn, well aware that it might destroy what remains of my mobility. But I rehearse the motion in my head, and when the time comes to carry it out, I do so without worsening the injury. The route of the run is straight ahead, but it looks completely different than it did just minutes ago. I almost slow at the sight, but I can't afford to with the beast's breath on my neck and—what is that? Hugo's sword tapping my shoulder? It's a tease. No, a command—*forward, faster.* I obey and, a few seconds later, exit the alleyway onto the route.

The crowds are gone. There's not even the usual detritus of beer cans, food wrappers, and vomit. But at least a dozen human corpses line the streets, some with fresh wounds— bright red blood, only just starting to crust into purplish- black. Other bodies are more decayed, muscles and guts exposed and graying. A couple are just skeletons with skull fractures.

But the human corpses are nothing compared to the hundreds of dead bulls piled up on all sides, mountains of meat and fur and bone. Some are all bone, bleached in the sun, while others still have all their flesh, eyes just beginning to cloud over. Every direction except the way I came is a barricade of carnage. I consider scrambling over one of the piles, but seeing that they're all at least twenty feet high, my chances of making it over are slim. I have no choice but to stop. My breath is asthmatic and iron-tasting, and I limp in a half-circle to greet my pursuer—the boy-become-man.

"What do you want?" I wheeze.

Hugo spins the sword, but there's no gleam in his eyes— he stares at the twisting blade seemingly without interest or playfulness. The bull looks similarly glazed over, possessing no rage, no life except for the rise and fall of breath.

"The d-d-dead have n-no d-desire," Hugo says.

He stares me in the eyes, and for the first time in my adult life, I drop my gaze. I see the shadow of his blade rise up, and for a moment I'm tempted to fall to my knees and beg for my life. But no, I must meet my fate.

Just as I imagine the blade plunging through my chest,

Hugo drops it. The metal hits the ground with the most deafening clang I've ever heard, reverberating through my whole body, threatening to rattle loose the fibers of my being. I squint my eyes shut, praying I can keep it together right as my knees collapse.

As soon as I fall, the ringing stops. Around me are the sounds of conversation, laughter, and music. I open my eyes and find myself back in normal Pamplona. No corpses. No vacant streets. But also no Hugo. None of the passersby helps me up or even seem to notice me, so I pick myself up, my ankle still ablaze.

The Plaza de Toros is a block away, and I can hear the crowd roaring as matadors face off against the bulls. The two tickets are still in my pocket. I take them out and stare at them. It's only a few seconds before I can look no longer. A bulge wells up in my throat, and a heat boils behind my eyes. I crumple the tickets and toss them to the ground.

I'm going home, alone this time.

FOR MY FINAL GIRL

Serena's operation took all of twenty minutes. Dr. Kemp —standing at least six-foot-five—forbade us from being in the room for it, so I watched through the window, squeezing Arnold's hand until it turned purple. Neither of us said a thing while the doctor attached the neurotransference device to Serena's head, grinning and speaking words to her that we couldn't make out—hopefully something comforting like "this might tingle, but I promise it won't hurt." He would've had to shave her for the operation, but Serena had just finished her final cancer treatment and was bald as the day she was born. She lay still on the operating table, never once flinching or crying out for us. At eight years old, she was already a pro at handling surgeries. Needles no longer made her squirm, and neither did waking up to railroad tracks of staples holding her chest together. I'd love to say her toughness made me proud, but seeing a child that young so unfazed by pain put a knot in my stomach.

Unlike the tumor removal, neurotransference was relatively noninvasive. Researchers first tested it on rats, fixing rice grain-sized electrodes to their skulls and transferring the correct path out of a maze to their brains. The rats navigated the mazes without so much as a single wrong turn, rewarded at the exit with tiny cheese plates—I'd seen it myself on CNN. When it became evident that neurotransference made information "stick" more effectively than traditional memory reinforcement techniques, the FDA cleared the way for human trials.

Unfortunately, neurotransference proved beyond the budgets of most families, so only the wealthy could afford it in lieu of traditional schooling for their children. It would have been out of our family's grasp, too, had it not been for the success of a desperate GoFundMe campaign. It raised enough for not only Serena's cancer treatments but also her neurotransference—a nearly instantaneous way to catch up on the year of school she'd missed. Arnold and I spent many nights awake watching the green fundraising bar inch to the right at a glacial pace. It wasn't until the bar reached its goal weeks later that we finally got a full night's rest.

Now, as the neurotransference was actually happening, Dr. Kemp sat at the computer and poured over a mess of readings that looked like nonsense. I squinted at the screen and asked Arnold if he knew what to make of it, but he just shrugged. We'd find out soon enough. Instead of staring at the computer, I watched Dr. Kemp, reading his facial expressions. Was that eye twitch the sign that something had gone wrong? Did that smile mean the operation had been a success?

Arnold must have sensed my anxiety because he rubbed my shoulder and whispered, "It's gonna be okay, Mateo. 99.976, remember?" The percentage of patients who went through neurotransference without any complications. But the fact that Serena developed a cancer affecting only .00002% of the population made it hard for me to relax.

Dr. Kemp emerged from the room just as my throat started constricting. I opened my mouth but couldn't form words. Arnold took over for me.

"Everything go okay?" he asked.

I felt his pulse accelerating where our hands touched. As much as he pretended to have a cool head in stressful situations, I'd been with him long enough to know he just hid his fear better than most. When he straightened his posture, standing taller than normal, it felt like an overcorrection.

"Yes," Dr. Kemp said. He gestured through the window at Serena, who was now sitting up and rubbing her eyes. "She may need to sleep when she gets home, but this is an outpatient procedure. Be sure to administer the comprehension test after she's had some rest. If there are any gaps in her knowledge, schedule a follow-up and we'll get it taken care of. But I'm confident she won't be missing anything. There might even be a little extra in that brain of hers."

He winked, handing Arnold the novel-sized comprehension test, his massive hands making it look more like a pad of sticky notes.

"You didn't give her the fourth grade curriculum, too, did you?" Arnold said, an edge creeping into his voice. "I told you, we can only afford—"

"Mr. MacEwen, I've done only as you asked. Nothing more. Your billing will reflect as such."

Dr. Kemp donned a sour smile. The man irritated me, but I figured he was just one of those doctors who'd dealt with so many patients' traumas that he had little compassion left to dispense.

Lingering in the doorway, he pulled out a tin of dusty-looking mints, each of which had been snapped in half.

"Would you like one?" he asked.

I shook my head, and Arnold straight-up grimaced. It was doubtful anyone ever took Kemp up on the offer. Still, the man only shrugged, popped half a mint into his mouth, and excused himself.

Arnold and I entered the operation room to get Serena. I kissed her peach-fuzz head, told her I was proud, and took her hand in mine. Sitting on the examination table, she was dead silent, and her limbs were slack as a cloth doll's. I worried she wouldn't be able to walk by herself. A nurse came in with a wheelchair, but Serena shook her head, so I wrapped my arm around her back for support while we made our way toward the exit. Soon, she began to outpace me and she pulled away. I let her go. After so many different procedures and decisions made on her behalf, it must have been nice to have a little independence, the freedom to ignore the receptionist's "goodbye, Serena" without parental reprimand.

———

AFTER A NAP LATER THAT AFTERNOON, Serena passed her third-grade comprehension test with flying colors, but even as she sped through the questions, her mind seemed miles away. I knew children struggling to focus on a boring test was nothing out of the ordinary, but rather than tuning out of the Montana state history section, it seemed like she was tuning in to something far more important, her sharp eyes fixed on the driveway leading up our house.

When she went to her room and Arnold and I checked her answers at the dinner table, I whispered that something seemed off. Arnold licked his thumb, turned to the last page of the packet, and tallied Serena's score before replying.

"What do you mean?" he asked. "She did great. I don't think she'll have much of a problem adjusting to fourth grade. Maybe a little social catch up, but you know . . ."

"That's not what I'm saying. She . . ."

I sighed. What use was it explaining myself when I had nothing concrete to back up a gut feeling? Arnold beamed, writing an "A+" on the scoring sheet and tearing it out to put on the fridge. It would go next to the letter declaring Serena officially cancer-free.

"I'm gonna check in on her," I said.

When I reached her bedroom door, I froze up, irrationally worried that she'd be dead when I entered. Everything I'd read about neurotransference indicated that it was safe, and even when it did have unintended side effects—nausea, cluster headaches, fatigue—it hadn't once proved fatal. But Serena could be an exception. I didn't bother knocking and instead swung the door open, knob denting the drywall. I winced at the intensity of my entrance, but Serena didn't seem to notice.

Her room was dark, and she sat facing away from me, bathing in the blue light of Arnold's laptop. While she normally used the computer to play video games, she had something else pulled up now. I couldn't tell what, so I moved closer. It was Google Maps. On the page, was a pin somewhere in the middle of Kootenai National Forest. We'd never been there as a family, and as far as I knew, Serena didn't even know how to pronounce, much less spell, "Kootenai."

"What you got there, girly?" I asked, trying my best to sound curious and not disconcerted.

Serena zoomed the map in farther, ran her fingers over the coordinates, and then tapped the screen.

"That's where she is."

A lump rose in my throat.

"Who? A friend of yours, or . . . ?"

"Jasmine Sutton."

I blinked several times, running through the roster of

Serena's former classmates. No Jasmines there, from what I remembered. I shifted mental gears to her third-grade history curriculum, wondering if maybe this person was a local historical figure I'd forgotten since my time in elementary school. But no, a blank there too. Still, the name seemed familiar.

"Who is she?" I asked.

Serena leaned back in her chair and chewed her lower lip. "I don't know," she said.

The hairs on my neck stood up.

"You hungry?" I asked, desperate to change the subject.

Serena nodded, still staring at the map.

"I'll get you something to eat."

It took some self-control to not sprint out of there, but as soon as I got to the hallway, I sped toward the dining room, nearly tripping over my feet. Arnold must have heard me because he ducked his head out of the kitchen, spatula in hand, something that smelled like garlic sizzling on a pan.

"Everything okay?" he asked. "I made some—"

"Do you know who Jasmine Sutton is?"

"Of course," he said. "That girl from Bozeman. She disappeared a few years back. Last place anyone saw her was— shit, was it a 7/11? Pretty sure we watched that doc about her."

A low static filled my ears, and the dining room chair almost toppled as I sat down too abruptly. Arnold tossed his spatula to the counter with a plastic smack and came to my side.

"Mateo, what's wrong?"

"Did you ever talk to Serena about her?" I asked.

"No, never," he said. "It would only give her nightmares. Hell, Serena even looks like that girl. I wouldn't want her to—"

"She knows. She knows her name and her—ugh, Jesus."

"Honey, what?"

I waved a hand through the air as if the gesture might explain what the hell was going on better than my words could.

"She says she knows where she is," I said.

"Where she's buried?"

"Why would she be talking about this?" I asked, leaning forward in the chair and raising up my arms. "How could she have—"

I sighed, swallowed hard. One crisis after another. One more patch of rot on Serena's childhood.

"Listen," Arnold said, rubbing my back. "Kids have big imaginations, and let's be honest. Were we there the whole time she was in the hospital? No. I mean, maybe when we left for work, she turned on the TV and—and saw something she wasn't supposed to see. Maybe that same documentary we watched. I don't know."

I massaged Arnold's fingers, squeezing them one by one —a meditation. "You're probably right," I said. "But I don't want her learning any more about it."

"I agree. And as for supposedly knowing Jasmine's location, Serena's probably just playing make-believe."

"That's some morbid make-believe."

Arnold kissed me, and we smiled at each other. Some of the tension melted off my back. There was no need to obsess over a problem that probably wasn't real. Serena was cancer-free. She was moving into the fourth grade. Maybe I could make room for a little optimism.

———

As I was cleaning the table before dinner that night, I picked up the neurotransference comprehension test and threw it away. Serena had already passed it, so there was no need to keep it around. But when it landed in the trash can, something caught my eye. Handwriting on the back cover—not Serena's or Arnold's. I picked up the test, brushing off some stray coffee grounds.

The note read, *For my final girl.*

I scratched my chin. As far as I could tell, the message meant nothing—the start of an abandoned letter?—but I wanted to know who had written it regardless. I had a hunch.

Rummaging through the filing cabinet, I found a document from the pre-op neurotransference appointment containing a list of resources and instructions related to the operation. It was Dr. Kemp's handwriting, smooth and rounded—more a script than a scrawl. I checked it against the message on the test, and the writing matched. Acid rose in my throat. I was about to toss the note back in the trash when I hesitated, then tucked it along with the pre-op report into the filing cabinet.

I gazed at the dinner table, strewn with two weeks' junk mail, numerous books, and a few cereal-crusted bowls. My desire to clean was quickly deteriorating as my mind wandered elsewhere. Arnold was still chopping vegetables for his signature stir fry, so I had time to kill before the table needed clearing.

I headed to Serena's room, this time opening the door gently. Serena was nowhere in sight, but Arnold's laptop was still on her desk. We had changed the parental controls that afternoon, so I had no worries about her doing nightmare-inducing research on Jasmine Sutton. But now, there were eight Google Maps tabs open, each with a specific set of coordinates. Like the first, two were in Kootenai while three were in Gallatin National Forest, and two more abutted the Missouri River. My fingers trembled as they hovered over the trackpad, and I pulled them away, worried that a nervous slip might accidentally close a tab.

Where was Serena? I hurried over to her bed, threw off the blankets, and found no one underneath them.

"Serena?" I said, the loudness of my voice startling me.

A rustling under the bed caught my attention. I bent down and lifted the purple bed skirt. She was there, shaking and sucking her thumb, a habit she'd supposedly abandoned two years back. I lay on the sour-smelling carpet and scooted under the bed as far as my body would allow, my legs sticking out.

"What's wrong?" I asked.

She spoke in a stutter, syllables tripping over themselves, and her wide eyes gleamed in the darkness.

"He's going to kill me soon."

———

WHEN I TOOK a day off of work to check out one of the Kootenai coordinates, I didn't tell Arnold. We'd been saving time off for a long-overdue family vacation—nowhere too far from Kalispell, but I could never complain about Glacier National Park. Of course, we'd already been away from our jobs plenty for Serena's various operations, so taking even one more day for myself meant a shortened family vacation later on. Arnold would be pissed, but it didn't matter. I had to know that Serena wasn't just letting her imagination run wild.

After I dropped her off at daycare, the drive up to the forest took about two-and-a-half hours. An audiobook about native plant gardening played the whole way there, but it went in one ear and out the other. I'd wanted to start a native plant garden for a long time and had been waiting for Serena to get healthy before I committed to it. Priorities change, though, and under these circumstances, I didn't give a shit what kind of fauna rabbitbrush attracted.

I got as close as possible to the GPS coordinates and parked on the side of a narrow dirt road, my car angled downward into a patch of nettles. I locked up and prayed I'd still have a phone signal three miles into the woods. There were no trails to guide me, but at least I wasn't competing for daylight, the sun still high in the sky and bathing the canopy in a golden halo. The most direct path to the coordinates was thick with poison oak, fallen trees, and soil soft enough that my boots sank an inch with every step. The slight slope upward also didn't help, and by the time I'd passed the first mile, I was already sweating bullets and swarmed with mosquitos. My phone still had a signal, though, and for that I was grateful.

But by mile two-and-a-half, my phone was close to dead and I decided to turn it off. As long as I kept going straight, there'd be no way I could miss the coordinates. I continued on for what felt like a long time, at one point startling a deer who skittered up the hill and made me jump too. Deer, of course, were the least of my wildlife concerns—in woods this rugged, bears were surely nearby. When, a while later, I worried I'd overshot the location, I stopped and turned my phone on again for a quick moment. The coordinates were just a hundred feet north. I increased my pace, tearing the arm of my button-up on a jagged branch and nearly tripping over a fox's den. The slope got steeper, my leg muscles threatening to become tree roots. But just when I thought they'd give out, I saw it right in front of me.

A dirt mound, raised, with less foliage than the surrounding ground. The sun beamed through the clearing, burning my forehead, and whether from that or the sight of the mound, I nearly fainted. My guts felt like liquid, and I pressed a hand against my stomach to keep myself from spilling the lunch I'd eaten along the way. I'd need all the energy I could get for the trek back.

When at last I felt steady, I turned around and headed to the car. I didn't need to dig up the mound to know what was there—*who* was there. Serena had already told me.

————

I PICKED up Serena from daycare, trying my best to keep smiling and draw attention away from my sweat-matted hair and muck-covered jeans. If she noticed, she didn't say anything, though I would've come up with a lie if she had. Her silence continued for the most of the car ride. Any question I asked about her day she responded to with either a shrug or a single word. Soon, she fell asleep, her head bobbing against the hot vinyl seat belt. I figured I'd carry her to bed once we got home, but without warning, her whole body lurched forward as she gasped herself awake. My foot hit the brake, purely on instinct. Was she having a nightmare? Could you even fit a nightmare into a five-minute nap? I didn't know, but she didn't fall back to sleep again, her eyes wide and unblinking for the rest of the car ride.

When we got home, I told Serena to go to her room until I called for her.

"You aren't in trouble," I said. "Daddy just needs to have a private conversation."

An older kid might have assumed I was having an affair, but Serena didn't even react. Just wandered off in the direction of her room, feet shuffling like a zombie's.

After her door clicked shut, I called 911 and told the dispatcher about the mound. Given its distance from civilization and any designated park trails, the dispatcher had plenty of follow-up questions, and I had plenty of answers. Or theories, at least.

"Dr. Richard Kemp is the man you need to talk to," I said, trying to keep my voice from cracking. "He's the neurotransference specialist at Kalispell Neurology Associates, and I'm certain he implanted the coordinates in my daughter's head during her operation."

"Listen," the dispatcher said, sounding about a second away from a world record-length sigh. "Think very carefully about what you say next. Making a false police report, especially for something as serious as this—"

"It's not a false police report. I'm telling you, the coordinates are very specific. They're pulled up on my husband's computer. And I didn't think they meant anything either until I"—I hesitated, unsure if what I said next would wrongfully incriminate me—"until I went to check for myself. Of course, I didn't dig up any, uh—"

"Okay, sir. That's enough for now. We'll send an officer your way and another to the clinic. Will you be at home for the next couple hours?"

"Yes, yes, absolutely," I said, wiping the sweat off my brow.

"Good. Stay there."

An officer arrived soon after, cocking an eyebrow at me as if surprised I wasn't wearing a tinfoil hat. Then he stepped into the living room, noticed Arnold's framed Bobcats jersey, and started talking basketball. I didn't know much about the sport except that scoring three-pointers was beyond my skill level, and it was hard for me to carry on the conversation with a serial-killing doctor on my mind. The cop probably knew this and was just wasting time until the other one visiting the clinic could confirm my story, but eventually he started asking questions about the case, documenting my answers on both a digital recorder and pocket notepad.

Soon, Serena poked her head halfway into the room, acting like she did whenever Arnold and I invited over dinner guests she'd never met. I thought about waving her away until the interrogation was over, but the cop overrode my authority and invited her to sit beside him on the couch. Perhaps he figured she'd say something that would prove me guilty of either murder or bullshit. I prayed I wouldn't spend the night locked up.

Arnold came home thirty minutes later. When he saw the cop sitting beside Serena and me, his face reddened. He set a bag of groceries on the ground a little too hard, splitting open a container of milk. After a minute of cursing and cleaning, he joined us in the living room, that crimson blush still plastered on his face.

As soon as I caught him up on what I'd done that day, he grew silent and small, easing back into his chair and blinking rapidly. I could tell he was angry at me, but not just me. He sat, mostly without talking, while Serena and I answered the cop's questions. Whenever they asked him something, they had to repeat it. Arnold was off in another world, dissociating from whatever nightmare he'd found himself in.

Finally, the call came in from the other cop. Dr. Kemp hadn't been in the office since Serena's neurotransference operation. When the cop searched his computer's neurotransference records, the coordinates were indeed there. An APB had been issued with a description of Kemp and his vehicles, and teams would be dispatched to check each of the eight sites that evening.

I was in the clear, no longer the implicit suspect in multiple child murders.

The cop got up from the couch and was about to head out when Serena spoke, her face half-burrowed in a cushion.

"He watches me sometimes," she said.

The cop stopped in his tracks. Arnold lifted his eyes for the first time since he'd sat down. We stared at each other, frozen.

When we snapped out of it, all the adults rushed to her room, Arnold and I leading the charge. I snapped on the lights. The cop checked the closet and under the bed. Arnold flung open the curtains and looked outside. It was his scream that almost made me fall over. If Arnold, of all people, was screaming, something was deeply, deeply fucked. Everyone swarmed the window.

Ghostly handprints, bigger than either Arnold's or mine, stained the glass. And below the sill, two massive boot prints faced us, the mud from last night's rain curled but not yet dried around the edges.

I bolted out of the room, convinced against all reason that Serena had been kidnapped in the minute it took us to investigate her room. But there she was, still on the couch, her knees folded up against her chin, tears streaking down her cheeks.

"I don't want to die," she said.

————

THE COPS NEVER FOUND KEMP. And even when the Feds entered the picture, they couldn't find a trace of him. Not even his car. You'd think a six-foot-five man would be easy to spot, but apparently not.

What they did find were eight bodies exactly where Serena said they'd be. Eight girls whose families now had long-overdue answers, but no real justice.

Serena turns thirteen next week. I still check her window every night, the yard as well. We even installed a motion-activated flood light and a security camera should someone try to sneak up under the cover of dark. So far, no one has.

But that's the thing. Sometimes I look at the security footage over my morning cup of coffee—skimming through the bits where nothing happens and stopping whenever a critter activates the light while dashing across the yard. And this morning, when I checked it, I saw something. Just out of the range of the light. Past the fat, lumbering possum, past the native plants garden taking up half our yard—a large shadow, darker than the night, and a shining pair of eyes, white and glinting.

I wonder if it's him, waiting for his final girl.

LOCKDOWN

No one understood why I transferred schools as a sophomore, especially given that I moved from the "best" one in town to one with almost as many dropouts as it had roaches. Sure, my new school had a better football team, but last I checked, girls couldn't try out. Even worse, none of my friends from middle school went there, and my hopes of making new ones were hampered by the fact that I transferred midyear. By then, everyone had already found their people and I was the outsider, the girl to gossip about but never actually talk to. *I bet she got expelled from Richmond. Probably did something real fucked-up.*

Of course, I could never tell anyone the real reason I left —not even my parents or my closest but quickly drifting friends. Nor could I admit that I'd literally seen it coming when Richmond High became the worst kind of national news. Some burdens are meant to be borne privately, even when they gnaw at your insides like rats in a cage of flesh.

The day I decided to transfer was the day Richmond held a lockdown drill. It happened in English, where I sat next to Leon Hoffman—yes, *that* Leon Hoffman. This was several months before anyone outside of Richmond High would come to know his name. Every day in class, he'd offer to help me with the opening grammar practice, resting his arm—decorated in Sharpied zig-zags and band logos—on my desk. I always told him I could figure out the grammar on my own, even though it was a lie half the time. Rejected, Leon would remove his elbow from my workspace, but he'd keep his desk close to mine, blocking me in for the rest of class. My desk had a bar on the other side, meaning I had to squeeze out on Leon's side to escape. He'd pretend not to know it was a tight squeeze, and I'd end up brushing against him, every hair on my body bristling. This claustrophobic wriggling meant I was often the last one out when the bell rang, left alone with Leon exactly as he intended. My desire to sprint out of the classroom was always strong, but I felt like a rabbit in the presence of a wolf, so I walked out of the room casually—no sudden movements, clutching my textbooks to my chest to hide the shakes. Leon would tail me every time, staying half-hidden in the hallway crowd and seemingly indifferent to the fact that his next class and mine were on opposite sides of the building. The first time he did this, I was sweating and breathing hard by the time I got to the chemistry room. Mrs. Kepnes asked if I'd just gotten out of gym. I said "yes" because lying was easier

This stalking routine continued for a full month, but it wasn't until the lockdown drill that Leon actually asked me out. That day, I could tell something was off from the way he stayed silent during grammar practice, bouncing his knee as he zeroed in on his own worksheet instead of mine. I briefly entertained the notion that he'd given up on me—that maybe I wouldn't have to request a new seat from Mr. Sands after all. But just as Mr. Sands wrapped up the grammar bell ringer and transitioned to a review of lockdown procedures, Leon scooted toward me and placed his clammy hand over mine.

Despite his flushed face, his words carried no inflection, no hint of shudder or shake.

"Go to homecoming with me," he said.

Behind me, a girl snorted. Leon didn't turn to glare at her; his eyes, pale blue and unblinking, were locked on mine. While grasping for the right response, I hoped Mr. Sands might yell at Leon for talking and cut off the conversation before I was forced to answer. But the man was deep in lecture mode about how "lockdown procedures have been proven to save lives in school violence situations."

"I can't." I cursed my choice of words and stared down at the profanity carved into my desk.

"Well, if you can't go to homecoming, you can still go on a date with me another time. What about today? You can come to my house."

I glanced at the girl behind me. She was biting her lip and staring at her phone but still clearly listening. I don't know what I expected from her, but whatever it was, I didn't get it. I was on my own.

"I don't want to," I said, and before he could respond, I raised my hand.

"Yes, Shaine?" Mr. Sands said, sighing as if I were a heckler interrupting his speech.

"Can I move to charge my laptop?" I pointed to a corner of the room as far away from Leon as possible.

"We're not using laptops today," Mr. Sands said. "And the drill is about to—"

On cue, the intercom's low chime sounded three times, then Principal Hurtz's voice announced the start of the lockdown. A boy in the back gave a fake scream, and his friends laughed.

"Cut it out," Mr. Sands said, then pointed to the boy. "Get the lights, Caidon. Everyone, move over that way and keep it down."

Leon had blocked me in again, his desk even closer than usual. When the lights went off, his eyes glinted at me like a predator in the night. Rather than asking him to move, I climbed over the metal bar on the other side of my desk, hoping the stretch wouldn't tear my jeans. I shuffled over to the wall with everyone else and took shelter under the Shakespeare poster featuring Hamlet holding a skull. Leon sat down beside me, his knee knocking against mine. Immediately, tightness seized my chest.

Around us, students whispered to each other and scrolled through their Instagram feeds. When Mr. Sands confiscated Caidon's phone, the rest of the students caught on and put theirs away, though they continued to talk.

"Quiet," Mr. Sands said. "Don't make me say it again."

"A shooter would still know we're in here even if we were quiet," someone said. I couldn't see who in the dark. "They're not stupid."

"Save it. Don't make me call home."

The student muttered something before falling into silence, and the rest of the class followed. For a while, the only sound was the rustle of fabric as students tried to get comfortable on the vinyl floor. With Leon staring at me and nothing to distract from it, my skin crawled. I tried to focus on my after-school plans—a trip to the mall with Ellen and Nevaeh. We planned to shop for homecoming dresses and be each other's platonic dates. Thinking about them made it easier to breathe, if only just slightly.

Then, Leon laughed. I glanced up from my lap and realized he was no longer looking at me. He stared off into the darkness, past rows of askew desks. In the far corner, separated from the rest of the group, was someone standing perfectly still. My eyes struggled to adjust to the darkness, and I could just barely make out the student's silhouette. Strangely, Mr. Sands hadn't yet hissed at them to join everyone else in the room's blind spot. I squinted to get a better look, and as my eyes adjusted, the student's—the girl's —clothes came into focus: tightly laced Chucks, cuffed skinny jeans, and a Post Malone T-shirt peppered with holes. Funny—I was wearing the same outfit. My gut twisted. Whipping my head around to check who else was seeing this, I discovered it was only Leon.

That's when Leon's smile started to fade. He blinked several times as his eyes went glassy. I looked into the corner again and all at once realized the holes in the girl's shirt weren't a fashion statement—they dripped with something wet, but whatever it was vanished before hitting the floor, like a snowflake melting mid-fall. The girl held a shaky hand over the biggest hole, and seconds later, her head slumped forward and into view. It was my head; the girl was me. As the holes in her torso leaked, her form became translucent, toes dissolving first and everything up to the neck following. Her floating head was the last to be swallowed up in nothing-ness, and by then, all life had drained from her eyes. She disappeared. I disappeared.

I remember what happened next only in flashes: Leon looking back at me with silent tears rolling down his cheeks; the thin whistle of my throat closing up; the sound of Mr. Sands's voice right in front of me.

"It's just a drill, Shaine," Mr. Sands said as someone turned the lights back on. "Breathe, Shaine, breathe. Every-thing's okay."

I spent that whole night sobbing into my pillow. My parents—having received Mr. Sands's email—sat on either side of me in bed, asking why the lockdown drill had upset me so much. I never answered them. There were plenty of moments between sobbing fits in which I could've said some-thing coherent, but what would they have believed?

They didn't let me transfer schools right away. But two

weeks later, after every teacher had called home about my declining grades and catatonic behavior, my parents finally agreed to send me to Willis High School.

For a while, Ellen and Nevaeh tried to keep in touch. They'd heard about my breakdown in English but didn't know the reason behind it. I thought about telling them, or at least telling Ellen; she actually believed in the supernatural. But our supernatural explorations were always just for fun—watching WitchTok videos to learn fun spells, or using a Ouija board to find boyfriends from beyond the grave. To inject the supernatural with life-or-death seriousness felt wrong, like I'd be killing one of Ellen's greatest sources of joy. I considered telling Nevaeh about my vision instead, but I knew she'd just laugh and call me a crackhead.

This vision wasn't just about me, though; the rest of the class could be in danger too. Had other students received visions? Seen projections of themselves riddled with bullet holes? Were they, like me, paralyzed into silence? These thoughts circled my brain like wolves. I couldn't focus in class. I couldn't hold a conversation. I couldn't sleep. But, if Instagram was to be believed, everyone else was just fine. Ellen and Nevaeh's Homecoming pictures proved they were doing well without me. They wore sparkly strapless dresses and beamed at the camera, brighter than I'd ever seen. I could never stare at these pictures for long without crying. They reminded me of how much I'd given up on account of, what—a hallucination? The more time passed, the less real my "vision" seemed. Maybe Leon hadn't seen anything. Maybe he'd just been staring into the corner and laughing like a weirdo. Maybe it had all been in my head and mine alone—a momentary psychotic break.

It took months for me to get there, and by then, I'd abandoned the idea of telling anyone about the experience. Little by little, I found myself able to complete homework again and even talk to my new peers when the teacher told us to "pair and share." Still, these peers weren't my friends, and I knew it was time to return to Richmond. On February 14, my parents filled out the transfer paperwork. That same day, the school's halls filled with thunder.

Leon's name appeared in every newspaper from the *Washington Post* to the *New York Times*. I wasn't mentioned in any of the articles, but another girl was—Hailey North. Not Ellen. Not Nevaeh. But that didn't make the news any easier.

I try not to blame myself for staying silent. I try to be thankful for the vision that saved me. But I think I'll be trying for the rest of my life.

TOP 5 GHOSTS CAUGHT ON CAMERA

Hey, come on in. Sorry about the mess. I had one too many last night, didn't really sleep, and, uh, here we are. Still glad to be on your show, though; my house is haunted as fuck. Here, let's get out of the living room. The lighting in here is terrible and, uh, well . . . Oh, sure, I'll take off the shell necklace—could get noisy on the microphone. Sound okay on your end? Great. Let's get this thing started. I think we'll only get through four of the ghosts. Wait, there's only enough budget for one shooting day? Cheapskates. Well, we'll get through at least a few and—okay. Yeah, I understand. They want all five. The show is called *Top 5 Ghosts Caught on Camera*, after all. I'll try to keep things trucking along, but no promises. The last one isn't that interesting, anyway. Oh, we're shooting now? Hell yeah. Can you toss me that beer?

FIVE—THE MAN IN THE PANTRY

This guy inspired me to get the camera in the first place. I had to be sure my eyes weren't tricking me, and the video proves they weren't. Look there—it's not a bug on the lens. See the baseball cap, the nose, the glasses? They must be sunglasses because I've never been able to see his eyes. Sometimes his body appears, too, but most of the time it's just his head floating in front of the canned goods. When I open the pantry door, he just hovers there and stares—not at me, though. At something, or someone, behind me. He's probably creeping on Number Three, but we'll get to her later.

I've had to reach through this guy a few times to get some soup, and it's like fisting a polar bear's asshole. I swear to God, there's frost on the can when I pull it through him. He never reacts to my touch, or if he does, it's not until after I've slammed the pantry shut and split.

Funny thing is, I can't find any death records for him. Three and Four died in the house, and two died just down the block by the gas station, but the man in the pantry is a mystery. Hell, maybe I should pass out "do you know this man?" flyers with stills from the footage. Might find someone who recognizes him and knows why he won't leave my goddamn pantry. But I can deal with him being there as long as he doesn't go all poltergeist on me. I don't want burst cans of chicken noodle leaking everywhere. Christ knows I'm messy enough on my own.

ONE—HER

What? No, that's not how countdowns work. We'll talk about the others first. You trying to scramble my brain?

FOUR—CADENCE HOWARD

Cadence was the previous owner of the house. Lived alone and died choking on a dog biscuit. Weird, right? She liked to know what her dog was eating—try it first, so the pooch wouldn't have to suffer through a fifty-pound bag of sawdust. That's what the neighbor said, anyway. Cadence Howard—cuckoo for fucking Cocoa Puffs.

There I go, railing on her again. No wonder she hides my socks. See, she and I got off on the wrong foot—ha! When I bought this place, the realtor warned me that Cadence still made some post-mortem appearances, and I used that fact to knock down the price. I was loud about it too. "180K for Amityville, here? Please! 140, or I'm out." Cadence heard me, of course. Didn't you, chica?

No, don't get up. She always throws things when I provoke her. Never anything breakable—just magazines and shit. The one time she hit me, it was with a *Bass Pro Shop* catalog. Harmless.

Oh, the footage? Yeah, of course. Most of the time she stays out of sight, but I've been lucky enough to catch her on the camera stationed in the nur—uh, that room.

On second thought, can we skip this clip? It's not that interesting, really. Just a little mist is all.

ONE—CAN YOU HEAR HER?

I don't hear a goddamn thing.

THREE—JOSIE HOWARD

Okay, okay, sorry. Let me get it together . . . all right. I'm good.

Let me ask you this: is it wrong to be turned on by a ghost? Hell, your face says it all. What should I expect, asking such a weird question? But hold up, I'll show you the footage.

She's a babe, right? Not some Hollywood ghost bitch in a

white nightgown. Fucking black leather booty shorts, see-through crop top, and a face that'd make an Instagram model cry. That's why I said Number Five might be creeping on her. I mean, who wouldn't?

Huh? Oh yeah, she OD'd. Got big into opioids after her mom choked to death. She came back from the bar trashed one night, shot up some fentanyl on the toilet, and never woke up. At least she gets to be with her mom here. It's funny, though; I'm not sure they're aware of each other's presence. I've never seen them appear together. Or maybe they're fighting. Yeah, I bet that's it. Given how batshit Cadence was, I don't imagine Josie paid her many visits. Cadence is probably pissed and—

Hey, quit—not the plates! Jesus, I've pissed her off now. Don't walk through the kitchen when you leave unless you want stitches in your feet.

Where were we? Oh, yeah. I guess it's just good Cadence died first. It's hard losing a parent—I know from experience—but it's even harder losing, well . . .

Hm, I need another beer. You know what, let's take five. I'll just clean the kitchen while I'm in there.

ONE—YOU HAVE TO

. . . I can't. I won't.

TWO—RAHI PAREKH

My stomach hurts. Why don't we call it day? . . . no? What do you mean we have to do it now? Can't you—

Okay. All right. Rahi Parekh. Thank God I barely knew the kid. His death would've broken my heart even more than it already did. I saw him at the skate park a couple times, and damn, that boy could tear up the ramp. He was, what, eight, nine years old? I called him "Tiny Hawk." He called me "old weird asshole." Little shit. What's wrong with a thirty-two-year-old man going to the skate park? I just wanted to see if I could still shred. I couldn't, but—

Oh, no, I have no idea why his ghost comes to my house. I mean, skaters love trespassing, so that might be it. Wouldn't be surprised if he ghost-skates through the neighbors' hallways too. I just hope he visits his dad, at least. Poor guy. If my heart hurts for anyone, it's for him. In fact, he and I met once at a parents'—well, never mind. It's not important.

Point is, give your kid a helmet and tell them to watch out for cars.

ONE—IT'S TIME

You should leave now. Like I said, I'm coming down with something. Could be contagious, you never know. And if Cadence starts acting up again . . . well, yes, I know I said she's harmless, but I lied to make you feel comfortable. She could sneak up behind you and—

Okay, okay, Jesus—let go of my arm. Goddamn. You're not going to leave, are you? Not until I tell you?

Give me a second to fuckin' breathe.

. . .

All right, here we go.

ONE—LAURA

We had her for five months before she . . . you know. Really, I lost Laura and Maggie both that night. Maggie couldn't accept my side of the story. Can't say I blame her, though. She was working third shift stocking shelves at the grocery store, so it was my job to look after Laura five nights a week.

I'd sit on the couch and play *Call of Duty* until Laura started crying, then I'd check to see if she needed a diaper change or a bottle. Maggie pumped before work, so there was always milk in the fridge. As long as Laura had a clean diaper and a full stomach, she'd chill out and I could keep gaming. So, yeah. Pretty easy job, right? Impossible to fuck up?

. . . What's that look for? You want me to relive this nightmare, but you're here sneering at me every step of—

Me, projecting? No, listen. Keep that fucking look off your face or I swear to God I'll—

Yes, yes. I'm breathing. I'm calm. No need for that.

It happened last October. Laura was lying underneath one of those baby activity gyms. You know what I'm talking about; it's shaped like a tent and has a bunch of plastic shit hanging from it that lights up and makes noise. This one was animal themed. Of course, I couldn't wait for the day we'd get rid of it—got sick of hearing "I'm Leo the Lion! Rawr!" two million times a day. Now, I'd fucking kill to hear that.

Oof. Give me a sec . . .

Okay, so Laura was playing with Leo the Lion, and I was playing *Call of Duty,* racking up a phenomenal kill streak. No one could touch me. Ten or so kills in, Laura started crying behind me. I didn't do anything about it right away, figuring her shit wasn't going anywhere and could wait until the end of the match. She wouldn't starve, either, if that's what she was crying about.

You've got that look again. Don't . . .

Yeah, so I kept killing these guys, and then Laura's crying turned to gurgling. I called out to her, all sweet-like, saying, "It's okay, baby. Daddy's coming. Just give him a minute." And then I went back to kicking ass, right on the precipice of victory. Then these guys started fucking mobbing me. After a couple minutes, I took them out—headshots, all of them—and things started to cool down again. The match clock was just about out, and my lead was big enough that I figured I could turn away without sacrificing my win. Only, sometime between those guys mobbing me and that moment of rest, Laura stopped making sounds. No crying. No gurgling. No "I'm Leo the Lion! Rawr!"

And, God, you're probably thinking I should have taken that as a sign to—you know what? Fuck retrospect. The point is, I didn't do anything. She was quiet, so I kept playing. And I played and played and played until Maggie got home. And then Maggie kissed Laura's cold, limp little head. And then Maggie screamed and screamed and screamed until her throat bled.

And now we're fucking here.

What? Yes, of course I hear her gurgling in the living room. I hear it every goddamn day of my life. I'll never not hear it. Not until I put a fucking bullet in my skull.

Is that what you wanted to hear? Are we done?

REMI ROOK THE CANNIBAL COOK

My sisters called me "Doorstep" growing up. Sure, there are nastier names they could've given me, but this one was personal. See, the doorstep is where my parents found me bundled in a Loony Tunes blanket, jaundiced as all hell and screaming my head off at two in the morning. Our night-owl neighbor, Mrs. Ainsley—the kind who sat on her porch with a pair of binoculars and jotted down license plate numbers—never saw anyone come or go that evening. All she remembered was my screech suddenly cutting through the hiss of prairie grass. Maybe she was dozing at her post when my deliverer came, but I doubt it. The old widow kept a vampire's sleep schedule. So it's a mystery who abandoned me. I used to entertain the idea that it was no one at all—that I simply sprung into existence out of a great nothing. But that couldn't be it. I must have come from *someone*.

When my parents adopted me—because what other choice did they have?—they already had children of their own. Brittany and Brooke were twins, and even though we were around the same age, we rarely played together. They came up with my nickname after our parents told them how I joined the family. And I'm not sure if it was Brittany or Brooke who said it first, but soon they were both laughing, pointing at me and chanting the name in that eerie unison only twins can achieve. Our dad sighed and left the room, while our mom stared at the girls, open-mouthed and stammering.

"Stop it!" she said. "Evan was a gift to this family, and I won't have you treating him—"

But I stopped listening; the glazed look in her eyes told me all I needed to know. I was the reason she worked over-time to put enough food on the table. I was the reason school kept calling with "concerns about your son's social develop-ment." I was the reason Mom and Dad whisper-shouted at each other long after they thought I was asleep. So yes, I was quite the "gift."

Whenever I was home I tried to stay invisible. I played with Legos in my bedroom, which used to be Dad's music room. Most often I built the houses I imagined my biological parents lived in, castle-high with fountains out front and fairy forests out back. Sometimes I'd act out scenes with Lego people, making my imagined parents' voices sound soft, kind, and delighted to see me. But I kept my volume low, convinced that if my adoptive family barged in on one of these moments, the magic would dissipate and never return.

There was only one time a week when my adoptive family felt exactly like my Lego family. Each Friday at dinner, we'd watch *Remi Rook the Cannibal Cook* on public access television, and for thirty minutes we'd all smile, laugh, and gasp together. None of us had a taste for human flesh, but Remi had a way of making cannibalism entertaining and even a little appetizing. Every adult in town had applied to be a meal on his show—willing to donate any body part that wouldn't be missed—but only a lucky few were chosen. Had the show been broadcast outside of Western Nebraska, it probably would've matched the popularity of shows like *Cheers* or *The Golden Girls*. But our little patch of flyover country was happy to keep Remi's show a proud and secret piece of our cultural heritage.

I remember my ninth-grade biology teacher, Mrs. Schultz, being on an episode and returning to school Monday with a chunk of her arm missing. She beamed as she spoke of Remi, gesturing wildly even as her stitches popped loose, blood spilling through the broken seam. She didn't seem to notice; Remi had the power to make people forget about their pain. But more important than forgetting the pain was the love that came to the show's guests. After Mrs. Schultz's TV appearance, students focused when she lectured, crowded her desk to chat with her after class, and even bought her Christmas presents. Being on Remi's show elevated her from the teacher whose name students forgot by senior year to the teacher whose class every student wanted to take. If going on the show had done this much for Mrs. Schultz, I had to wonder what it could do for me. Would it make my sisters less likely to call me "Doorstep" and my parents more likely to smile when I walked through the door? The idea was worth a shot.

Of course, as a fifteen-year-old, I couldn't put my name in Remi's hat just yet; the state of Nebraska frowned on cannibalizing minors. But not willing to wait that long, I scraped together seven months' worth of allowance to buy a fake ID. Jacob Masters, the junior who sold that sort of thing, was even less inclined than my other classmates to talk to me, but as soon as he saw my stack of cash, he grinned like a hyena and rubbed his hands together. It was easy as that.

While my family attended church regularly, I had never

felt any special affinity with God. Still, I spent the next few weeks praying I'd get the call from Remi. I checked the answering machine every day after school to see if he'd left a message, but the only messages we ever got were from teachers complaining about my sliding grades. I erased those ones, not concerned about my parents yelling at me so much as the answering machine filling up before Remi could leave a message. Had I missed his call, I'm not sure if I would've discovered the truth about myself.

The call came on a Saturday, six days before the next live show. I'd just gotten home after rollerblading around the neighborhood. While I'd intended to be out longer, crashing after hitting a curb cut my blade time short. My skinned knee wasn't bloody, but it sure as hell hurt, so I tried to take my rollerblades off without causing further injury. Across the living room, my mom shredded junk mail and my dad folded laundry. When the phone rang, neither of them got up. Immediately nervous, I froze in place, one rollerblade strapped on and the other still resting on the shoe rack. Dad called for Brittany or Brooke to get the phone. The twins didn't appear after four rings, which was when my dad remembered his third child.

"Evan," he said, not even looking at me. "Could you get that?"

I lurched across the carpet, dragging my single rollerblade behind me, and sprung for the phone. In my haste to pull it off the wall, I thought I accidentally hit the switch hook and hung up. But when I lifted the phone to my ear I heard soft static instead of a dial tone.

"Hello?" I said, my voice cracking. I cleared my throat.

It was silent for a moment before a familiar voice rumbled into being. The man sounded Southern and exuded down-home hospitality.

Strangely, I don't remember what Remi said other than that I'd been selected for his show. What I remember was the feeling of hot, ecstatic pressure in my skull. It took tremendous effort not to scream and jump and probably break my rollerblade-bound ankle. I hadn't told my parents about my show application, and they didn't pay enough attention to notice my behavior changes—pacing, jumpiness, insomnia—leading up to Remi's call. Little did they know, they were living under the same roof as a superstar, and I wasn't about to let the secret out yet. They'd find out when the episode aired live.

The wait until Friday felt like a decade. I napped in class to make time go faster, and the second I got home I rewatched the episodes of Remi's show my parents had recorded to VHS. I took notes on how guests introduced themselves in order to prepare my own introduction, and when Remi's "Rate My Flesh" segment came on, I prayed that he'd rate mine highly. It was rare for him to dislike a person's taste, but when it happened, locals treated that person like they were cursed, rotting from the inside out.

When Friday finally came, I told my parents I had a study group. If Brittany or Brooke had said the same, Dad might've asked where they were going, who would be there, and what time they'd be back, but for me, he gave a grunt in the affirmative without looking up from his book.

I left the house dressed in my Sunday best: white button-up, blue tie, and gray slacks. Maybe not the ideal outfit to be cannibalized in, but I wouldn't dare dress down. Since I had no car I biked the ten miles to the TV station, flying down darkening dirt roads, past cornfields and rusted-out mailboxes askew in their posts. The TV station was a monolith on the horizon, broadcast tower jutting into the pink autumn dusk. By the time I reached it I was soaked in sweat, and I cursed myself for putting nice clothes on before the ride instead of after. I pushed through the station's glass door anyway, my heartrate escalating despite the bike ride being over.

Inside the station, half the fluorescent lights were off, and I couldn't tell if it was to save electricity or because they were dead. The gray carpet was frayed and pilling, but even with its wear, it soaked up all sound, leaving an eerie silence. I shuffled up to the reception desk, and seeing no one around, took a second to tame my sweat-plastered hair.

At that moment, a light went on above a doorway down the hall. Bright red, it said On Air. My breath caught inside me, and I didn't know what to do. Was Remi starting the recording without me? Had I arrived too late and been replaced by the missing reception desk worker? Just as I was starting to spiral, Remi opened the studio door and walked out, seven feet tall and tanned as leather. I exhaled, and it must have been loud, because the man chuckled and held out his hand to me.

"No need to be nervous, young man," he said, his voice sounding just as it did on TV but so much fuller in person— even the muffling carpet couldn't steal its richness. "Evan, right?"

"That's right," I said, my throat dry and palm wet as I shook his hand.

"Well, it's a pleasure to meet you . . . and eat you."

He laughed at his own joke like a dad would. It filled me with calm, and for a moment I pictured Remi as my father. I didn't have long to entertain the thought before the man led me to the studio, his giant, gentle hand cupping my shoulder.

"Here's where the magic happens," he said, opening the studio door. "I know it's musty, but it's a second home. I don't cook for myself at my actual home, if you can believe it.

Just toss a frozen dinner in the microwave or pour a bowl of cereal."

I couldn't tell if he was kidding, but if he was he didn't laugh at the joke this time. Instead he pointed to the camerawoman cleaning a lens.

"That's Barbara," Remi said. "She's great. Been with me these seven years."

I wanted to ask what he meant by "been with"—I had a hard time picturing a married cannibal—but he kept going before I could ask.

"Not only is she great behind a camera, she'll also stitch you up once she's done filming. You're not allowed to quit, Barb. Too damn useful!"

She looked up from polishing the lens and smiled at Remi, folding her fists into a heart across her chest. Then she walked over to me and cradled my hand between hers. A tingle traveled up my spine.

"You won't bleed out on my watch," Barbara said, her eyes wide and serious. "No one ever has, and no one ever will."

I nodded, letting out a breath I hadn't realized I was holding in.

"Okay, Evan—what are we eating tonight?" Remi asked, taking his Stetson hat off a hook on the wall and placing it on his head. "Finger? Toe? Bicep? Nothing obscene, of course. Station won't even let me make rump roast."

"Uh, arm," I said, a tremble in my voice—it was happening, really happening.

"All right, all right—whole arm? Left one?"

I nodded, then nodded again, my head feeling too light.

"Great—go big or go home," Remi said, pulling a clipboard off a table. "Sign here, son."

Son. He really called me that.

A few giddy, chicken-scratch signatures later, I handed the clipboard back.

Remi checked his watch, which was set in a snakeskin band. "Hot dog!" he said. "Three minutes to showtime. Imagine if you'd refused to sign those papers. I'd've had to eat poor Barbara."

"Not here, but you can eat me all you want at home," she said, winking.

I turned away as Remi and Barbara shared a wet, smacking kiss. All the while, the studio's analog clock moved onward, closer to show time. I tapped my toe, and just when I thought Remi would never break off the kiss, he came over and led me to the stage.

The kitchen was nothing like the bigger cooking shows' luxury setups with a dozen sponsored, state-of-the-art appliances. No, Remi kept it simple—all part of his thrifty charm. Atop the table were three knives: a cleaver, a boning knife, and a chef's knife. A mutilated wooden cutting board sat beside them, and next to that was the gas stovetop and a cast-iron skillet. A minifridge was tucked under the table to store whatever non-human ingredients Remi intended to pair with my arm.

Just before we started filming, Barbara approached me with a syringe. I unbuttoned the cuff of my shirt and rolled it up for her.

"You're way ahead of me," she said, smiling as she injected the anesthetic into my arm. "Should kick in before Remi amputates, but if it doesn't, throw up a peace sign and we'll stop the show. Don't want you in pain up there."

"Thanks," I said.

Barbara took out a cotton ball to clean the puncture site, but she frowned upon discovering there was no blood. It was perfectly clean—nothing unusual, according to my family's doctor. In his words, I had "literal thick skin." Barbara pocketed the cotton ball, shook her head, and gave me a pat on the arm.

"You'll do great," she said, returning to the camera. "Just smile real big."

When the show went live, I waited offstage while Remi delivered his opening monologue. He stood in front of a banner that spelled out the show's name in cartoonish viscera. As usual, his monologue was packed with cannibal puns, declarations of love for his fans, and stomach-rumbling sound effects as a sort of dinner bell. It was after these rumbles that he ushered me onto the stage, accompanied by Johnny Cash's song "One Piece at a Time," which Barbara had cued up. I was lucky I didn't pass out from panic then and there, and as soon as I reached the kitchen table, I clung to it like a life raft to keep myself from fainting. My arm was starting to go numb. To make matters worse, Remi reached over to shake the hand it was attached to. Somehow, I kept myself steady enough to return the handshake.

"Evan Daniels, what a pleasure!" he said, then looked down at my hand in mock surprise. "Nice firm grip, young man. You give the shake, I'll give the bake. How 'bout it?"

Remi could've smiled at the camera then, really hammed it up, but instead he looked at me with those kind, crinkled eyes. I couldn't feel my hand in his—totally numb now—but I exhaled, my nerves settling.

"Good to meet you, sir," I said, my voice so soft that I wondered if the mic still picked it up.

"Tell us something about yourself, Evan."

"Um." I realized I couldn't mention being in high school —though it'd feel wrong to lie to Remi. "I like to rollerblade."

"Well, it's a good thing we're not cooking your leg tonight!" He smiled at me again, radiating an unexpected gentleness. "You ready, son?" he asked.

He lifted up my numb arm and let it drop like dead weight. I couldn't feel it—not the air rushing through my fingers nor the impact as my hand smacked the table. This being my first experience with anesthesia, I laughed. My shoulders relaxed. I was starting to forget about the camera, a dim silhouette just beyond the bright stage lights.

"I'm ready, sir," I said, closing my eyes and grinning like an idiot.

From there, I mostly remember the tiny fibrous pops as Remi sliced back and forth through my arm. I didn't watch for fear that I'd lose my nerve and run off stage, arm hanging by a hinge.

But Remi stopped halfway through. Normally he'd narrate to the camera while he made the cut, commenting on the "beautiful marbling" of his guest's flesh. I waited for what felt like minutes, but Remi didn't cut any farther. I could sense he was still beside me, but I could no longer hear him breathing. Feeling a sensation like heartburn bubble up inside me, I opened my eyes.

Remi's jaw hung wide open, his dentures slowly sliding out of place. I wondered what had gone wrong. Had my flesh somehow made the cannibal nauseous enough to stop? I doubted it. In all the episodes I'd watched, Remi had never done anything but smile and speak in soothing tones while amputating a guest's limb.

Then, behind the camera with her eye glued to viewfinder, Barbara said, "What in the pig-fuck hell?"

Barbara and Remi were staring at the same thing. I followed their gaze to my arm. Remi had only sliced halfway through it, but the wedge of exposed flesh didn't look as expected. In fact, there was no flesh at all beneath the skin. Inside was a great black nothing, a void that seemed to dim the studio's light. Shaking, I reached my other hand over to touch it but stopped just short, worried the cut might swallow me like a black hole. Had I been able to breathe, I would've been screaming.

Remi must have noticed my mounting panic because he rolled his shoulders, composed himself, and went on talking to the camera as if this were a cause for curiosity rather than terror.

"Well, folks," he said. "Can't say this is something I've seen before. I'd venture to guess you haven't, either, from the way you're looking, Evan."

I stared at Remi, hoping the sight of him would get my lungs working again. Or were they lungs? Did I even have those inside me?

Remi half-smiled and placed a hand over my unmutilated arm. He raised his head as he inhaled and then lowered it for the exhale, again and again, guiding me out of my strangled terror. Soon I could breathe once more, if only shallowly. Remembering the camera, I turned to Barbara.

"Shut it off," I said, my voice little more than hiss. Seeing Barbara frozen in place, I repeated myself, finding enough air to make it louder this time. "Shut the camera off!"

Barbara fumbled to put on the lens cap, missing it once, twice, three times. With each second the recording continued, I pictured my family at home, no longer cheering for me but averting their eyes and scrambling to turn off the TV. Maybe they'd change the locks before I got back—no entry for monsters.

Finally, the lens cap clicked into place.

A silence choked the set, and I found myself wondering if my insides were siphoning away the sound just as they had the light. When the silence became unbearable, Remi spoke.

"Listen," he said, his words clear and calm. "This might not be the way you imagined tonight going, but let me reassure you that it made for damn good television."

I snorted, unable to help myself, and again glanced down at the hollow within me.

"I don't think I can go back home," I said. "My family—"

Barbara hustled over to me and led me off the stage before I could finish the thought.

"No, no," she said. "Let's get some air."

When we left the TV station, it was cold out. A brisk wind blew dead leaves across the parking lot. The stars shone brightly, and I thought about the darkness inside me snuffing them out one by one—a greedy, insatiable thing. Barbara rubbed my shoulder in slow circles, and Remi stood on my other side, gazing out into the night. In a nearby cornfield, a fox yipped.

"It's a beautiful evening," Remi offered.

"I'm a monster," I said.

"Nonsense. That . . ." he gestured at my arm vaguely. "Well, I don't know what the hell it is. But it's interesting. No need to feel ashamed about being interesting. Most folks are about as interesting as a Lutheran church service. Even the ones who taste good."

"Yeah, I guess." I smiled, but it faded when I glanced at my wound again. "I don't like looking at it."

"Here," Barbara said. "How 'bout I stitch you up and Remi microwaves you a TV dinner? You can sleep on our couch."

"I can't," I said, feeling a bloodless blush flood my cheeks. "I have to—"

"C'mon, son," Remi interrupted. "You've had quite the night. And it's no trouble, really. Let us do this for you."

I considered it a moment longer and wondered why I was hesitating. This man was my hero. Barbara was, too, even if I'd only just met her. I thought about how different they were from my family, and my mind returned once more to the uncertainty that awaited me when I got home. Would they welcome me back? And more importantly, would I *want* them to welcome me back?

I was silent long enough for Barbara to notice.

"Well," she said. "You in?"

I knew how I'd feel if I said "no," how that feeling would stick to me like tar to a smoker's lung. It'd be with me for as long as I lived.

So I nodded.

And despite the void inside me, I felt warm.

MY BETTER HALF

How you determined which was my "gay half" and which was my "straight half" is a mystery to me. I suspect the realization came during last night's date at Texas Roadhouse. A handsome waiter approached our table, black T-shirt highlighting the bulge of his pecs, tight jeans highlighting a bulge of a different sort. I tried not to stare, but I must have grinned—or half of my face must have grinned. The gay half. You ate in silence, spreading cinnamon butter over the dinner rolls with enough force to flatten them into dense discs. I asked you what was wrong, but you said nothing. When I pressed the issue, all you offered was, "Long day at work. And the chicken here sucks." Our waiter came with the check. You didn't leave a tip.

"What was that?" I asked, brushing past the birthday saddle as we rushed into the parking lot. "If you're mad at me, don't take it out on the waiter. Seriously, what the fuck?"

We reached the car, and as you unlocked it, you smiled at me.

"Everything will be fine in the morning. Don't worry about it," you said.

I didn't know what to make of the mood swing, so I stayed quiet for the ride home.

————

I AWOKE the next morning in two places—my straight half in bed with you, and my gay half locked in the closet. A little on the nose, don't you think? It was disorienting, seeing two sights at once—a split screen of a spinning ceiling fan on one side and a pile of sweaty gym clothes on the other. Oh, and blood—the one consistent element holding both sides together. A crimson spray on the bedroom ceiling and a brown crust on the closet carpet. An absolute mess.

You rolled over in bed and smiled at my straight half. Even splattered with gore, your blonde curls were gorgeous, somehow immune to bedhead. You kissed my half-mouth, and when you pulled away, a thin web of blood went with you. You looked unbothered. Unbothered by any of this.

"How would you feel about a little . . . you know?" you said, massaging my torso with your soft, warm hands.

I shook my head, unable to speak. When your smile persisted, I shook more vigorously, stopping only when half of my brain almost dislodged itself. Your face darkened and you stroked your chin, whispering something indecipherable. A moment later, you grabbed my straight half and lugged me over to the closet where my gay half lay. Maybe you'd been wrong about which half was which. You switched out sides, locking the closet behind you.

Again, you put the moves on, your tongue tracing my neck, a sensation I normally loved but could no longer tolerate. I tried to twist away and, hell, I even thought about biting you—half a mouth could still do some damage. But I didn't. That wasn't my style. And frankly, I would have pissed myself if my bladder weren't cut in two. Everything inside had already drained out.

You must have seen the look on my face because you stopped again, this time gritting your teeth. For a second I thought you might kill me, fed up with trying to guess which of my sides was which, your experiment a total failure. And of course it was, but my reasons for thinking so were certainly different than yours. I didn't say that to your face, though. Who knew how you'd react?

Time was what you needed. Time to think, to hypothesize, to scheme.

"I'm late for work," you said, hopping out of my lap and stomping away.

The hiss of hot water came from the bathroom. I eyed my phone, pondering who I could call before you got out of the shower, but you stepped back into the room almost immediately to grab a towel. You tracked my eyeline, grabbed my phone, shattered it against the floor. I couldn't see where it landed, but I was sure it was in multiple places, just like me.

With no way to contact anyone, I waited until you left, practically catatonic. You'd probably be back for lunch— wouldn't trust me on my own for a whole day—so I had to make the most of what little time I had.

Half of me shuffled to the edge of the bed while the other half scooted against the back of the closet wall. Together, we stood up, slowly and precariously, balancing on one foot each like fucked-up flamingos. We hopped to each other, standing on opposite sides of the locked door. The thing was easy enough to open—just a twist of the lock—but in our rush, our bedroom half tripped. Barely catching ourself on the doorframe, a lung popped out and swung like a pendulum from my gaping cross section. We got that half of ourself upright again and tucked the thing back in.

Door open now, my halves met, and we hugged. *I* hugged. My closet half reached down to grab the sewing box, then both my halves hopped over to the bed. There, I spent the next couple hours sewing myself together, glancing at the clock every other stitch. When the spool ran out, I unraveled thread from the pillowcases, using those to finish the job. The colors weren't uniform—white becoming green—but that was fine. It was only a temporary solution. What a permanent one looked like, I had no way of knowing.

The moment of truth came when I stood up. There was a sound like fabric stretching as the slack between the stitches widened, my halves threatening to separate once more. But after a moment of me staying perfectly still, the seam didn't stretch any farther. Sure, someone could slip a spaghetti noodle through my center, but for now, the fix was stable enough.

I checked the clock. 11:58. You'd be home soon. I ran out of the room and down the stairs, my steps only semi-coordinated, the stitches at risk of tearing away if I slipped. But I made it out the front door, past the driveway, into a pile of bushes just as your car whipped around the corner like a drag racer's. I paused to breathe, my lungs inhaling at different times, losing some oxygen through the slit in my windpipe. You slammed the car door, hustled into the house. But it wasn't long before you stormed back out, screaming my name. I stayed hidden and didn't dare answer.

When it was close to one, after nearly an hour of pacing and shouting, you drove off again. Back to work so your boss wouldn't get mad. You'd deal with this when you got home. Or so you thought.

But I made sure you'd never find me. Where I went, I won't tell you. Just know that it wasn't with the handsome waiter from Texas Roadhouse. Though, if it were, I hope he'd never try to cut parts of me loose.

This is goodbye, not from one half of my being, but from a united whole—hurt, but healing.

THE REVEAL

J acob and Emily posted the gender reveal party event on
Facebook knowing full well there'd be critics. But that
was all part of Jacob's strategy for raising their child.
Anyone who criticized the event would no longer have a
place in their child's life. Without any Subaru-driving aunts
or NPR-donating high school friends whispering lies, it'd be
easier to keep their child on the right path.

Still, Emily initially objected to Jacob's idea, preferring a
private event page with a few select guests to a public one
that all could see, screenshot, and share in outrage. This was
Emily's inner Midwesterner, used to handling conflict with a
too-wide smile and a swift change of subject. But eventually
she accepted Jacob's idea, under the condition that he would
be the one to deal with the online backlash.

A dozen unfriendings and twice as many RSVPs later, the
day of the party arrived. They could've just revealed the news
on social media, but an announcement as important as this
one deserved more pomp and circumstance. As Jacob put it,
"When my business moved to a new building, we had a
ribbon-cutting ceremony. It'd be a shame if I put more flair

into that than the birth of my own child." Emily joked that childbirth did have a ribbon-cutting ceremony of sorts with the umbilical cord; Jacob only frowned in response. Such jokes frequently popped into Emily's head, but after two years of marriage, she'd mostly learned to keep them to herself.

The party took place in Redwood National Park, where Jacob had camped with his father countless times before he passed. When Jacob spoke about the place, he described it as "a church grown straight from the earth." Emily smiled whenever Jacob talked this way, but any time she called him a poet, he got red in the face and insisted poetry wasn't for him. It was too bad. Emily's college boyfriend had embraced his poetic side without shame, leaving love notes under her windshield wipers between classes. Had he not left those notes on other cars, too, Emily might have married him instead of Jacob. She tried not to think about it.

After a two-hour drive deep into the heart of the park, Emily and Jacob pulled into a campsite surrounded by three-hundred-foot wooden sentries. Golden light glinted through the canopy, and craning her neck upward made Emily dizzy. Seeing her sway, Jacob rushed over and placed his hands on her hips.

"The baby upsetting your balance?" He glanced down at her round belly.

"No," Emily said. "I'm light as a feather."

"We'll see about that!"

Jacob grinned, lifted his wife into the air, and spun her around.

"Stop! Please!" Emily said, smiling and laughing, at least for the moment.

Jacob let her down and kissed her on the forehead. "Hmm, you might not be light as a feather, but I'm strong as an ox."

Before Emily had time to either take offense or compliment his poetry, a truck pulled up, honking and flushing some birds out of a nearby bush. Emily and Jacob waved as the truck came to a dust-kicking halt right next to their car. Emily's parents, Ernest and Maureen, stepped out, grinning. Jacob embraced Emily's mother, then shook hands with her father.

"We come bearing gifts," Maureen said, poking her head into the truck's back seat to pull out two bags—one blue and one pink. "Of course, you'll only get one of these bags. I saved the receipts for both depending on which one I need to return."

"Maybe you can just hang on to that other gift," Jacob said. "Emily and I are hoping to have another sometime next year."

Emily opened her mouth to say something, struggling to remember ever having this conversation with her husband, but the arrival of another car put that thought on hold.

Before long, twenty other guests had arrived. Jacob waited an extra five minutes before deciding the party could go on without the ones still "lost in the woods." Everyone got to work setting up the tablecloths, disposable dishware, and potluck entrées that had sat in cars for too many hours. Jacob led the group in grace, then invited everyone to load up their plates—ladies first, of course.

Emily stood at the front of the line, serving herself a scoop of warm egg salad, a watery helping of wedding weenies, and several cubes of palest-pink watermelon. Her stomach wasn't rumbling, but she knew if she didn't eat, her mother would remind her of the baby's nutritional needs. Emily would pick at whatever looked edible and leave the rest for the birds.

When everyone had a full plate, Jacob sat beside Emily and across from his best friend, Garrett. The two men quickly got to talking about their Fantasy Football league, ignoring everyone else around them. On Emily's other side, her father scolded her mother for not packing any bug spray. When their argument somehow moved on to the topic of the best time for scheduling Ernest's knee replacement, Emily stood up to leave.

"Where are you going, Em?" her mother asked, only now noticing her.

"Getting another plate," Emily said, offering a flat, lippy smile.

"If you get any cornbread, don't put honey on it, dear. It can give babies botulism and—"

"I know, Mom. You sent me the article."

"Well, excuse me for reminding you!" Her mother held up her hands and immediately returned to discussing Ernest's surgery.

Jacob was still locked in conversation with Garrett, defending his choice of running back. He didn't even look up when Emily left the campsite.

Wandering past the buffet tables, Emily dawdled on her way to the outhouse. Sure, she needed to pee, but a little quiet and some air that didn't smell like egg salad were even greater needs. Inside her, the baby kicked, the swell of a foot briefly visible under her green dress. She smiled, then realized she was crying. If anyone saw her like this, she would've told them they were happy tears—nothing to be concerned about—but even she wasn't sure which feeling brought them on.

Questions that she normally tried to banish swirled around her head. *What if the baby comes out stillborn? Will Jacob and I get divorced? Will I be happier? Will I finally get to finish my English degree?*

A laugh, high-pitched and jackal-like. Emily froze, squinting ahead to see who or what was there. Just about anything could hide behind a redwood tree: a mountain lion, a bear, even an elephant. But this sounded like none of those creatures. The laugh echoed between the trees longer than a natural sound should, bouncing back and forth without losing sonic force. For a moment, Emily wondered if she was experiencing a sudden, strange episode of tinnitus or a side effect of pregnancy she'd never heard of before.

Then she saw the horns—two poking out from behind a tree, at least a yard long each, black but veined with glowing red cracks. Bits of ash drifted around the points, or maybe they were just gray floaters in front of Emily's eyes; she couldn't tell. But whatever they were, she was getting the hell out of there, full bladder be damned. She turned heel and rushed back to the camp, panting under the baby's added weight. The hairs on her neck stood up while the echoing laugh followed her, but as soon as she passed back into the camp the sound cut off like someone had pressed a Mute button. She almost stopped to look back, but figuring it might be a trip, she continued running in spite of her heart palpitations.

When Jacob saw her, he stopped talking to Garrett and jogged over. Everyone else turned to look, too, their conversations snuffed out instantly.

"What's wrong, honey?" Jacob asked, putting a hand on Emily's sweaty back. "You see a bear?"

"No," Emily said, out of breath and forcing a grin. "Just getting some exercise."

Jacob removed his hand from her and shook his head. "You know you can't do that," he said. "It's bad for the—"

"Yes, yes, I know. Can we just get to the reveal, please?"

Jacob sighed, took a step back, and turned to the onlookers. "Hormones, am I right?" he said, holding up his hands and smirking.

A couple guests rolled their eyes, but most laughed;

Emily wasn't sure if this laugh or the strange one from earlier was worse. Her cheeks burned red, and she shuffled over to the dessert table where she could occupy herself with food instead of conversation. She glanced down at a half-eaten cherry pie swarming with flies, grimaced, and turned her attention to the forest instead. A dark shape lurked behind a bush thirty feet off, but when she squinted to get a clearer view, nothing was there. A shudder passed through her. She closed her eyes, breathed deep, and pictured her favorite spa in the city. Relaxing and totally artificial—no strange animal sounds or stalking creatures to speak of.

In the meantime, Jacob prepared the gender reveal device, which he'd modified at home to maximize its pyrotechnic spectacle. The canopy was a few hundred feet above them, and assuming his calculations were right, the thing wouldn't go that high. If it shot up past the canopy, no one would be able to see the color when it exploded. After Jacob had it positioned correctly and made sure there were no park rangers around itching to write a ticket, he cleared his throat and gestured for everyone to come in close. The guests approached him. Emily lingered at the dessert table, and it was only Jacob calling her name that drew her out of her mental spa.

With everyone gathered, Jacob began his speech, feet spread wide and hands folded together. Emily knew that Jacob called this his "power pose"; he whipped it out whenever he brought his employees in for a meeting or a talking-to.

"I've gathered you all here today to celebrate new life," Jacob began, sounding as if he were reading from a teleprompter. "Emily and I have been blessed with a child. A child that we didn't always think would come."

Emily looked at her feet and tried not to cry. She'd asked Jacob multiple times to cut this part out of his speech.

"For the first six months of our marriage, we thought Emily was infertile," Jacob continued.

Emily balled up her fists, trembling, and her ears rang once more with that otherworldly laughter she'd heard by the outhouse. She whipped her head around to see where it was coming from, but no one else seemed to notice the sound. The too-intimate details of Jacob's speech had them transfixed. But the mix of her husband's over-rehearsed words and the incessant cackling overwhelmed Emily's senses. Jacob recounted, in agonizing detail, their appointments with multiple fertility doctors: first to the eighty-two-year-old Dr. Lawrence Albrecht, then to the young and leering Dr. Mitch Sampson for a second opinion. Jacob also mentioned their nightly pre-copulation prayers aimed at bringing sperm and egg together through divine intervention. While he'd prayed to God, Emily had cast a wider net, praying to any being that could bring them a child. Jacob preferred a strictly Christian approach, but he admitted to the crowd that sometimes the end justified the means.

With each new word that spilled from Jacob's mouth, Emily felt her temperature rise. She was a pressure cooker about to blow, and soon she could take the feeling no longer. In a sudden burst of motion, she shoved through the crowd.

"Honey, what—" Jacob said, moving to intercept her and then stopping in case she was about to puke from morning sickness.

But Emily wasn't sick. No, she was headed for the gender reveal device. She snatched the lighter from the ground, flicked it to life, and lit the device's fuse. The sooner this thing went off, the sooner she'd be able to go home. Jacob staggered forward, yelling, but stopped halfway to the device, seeing that he wouldn't make it in time to stomp out the fuse. Emily backed away but tripped and fell. Her father shouted out behind her, but as the man ran to help Emily, he slipped, too, his bad knee the culprit. The rest of the guests scrambled to help the groaning old man up, and Jacob ran toward Emily, cursing the whole way.

The device went off, booming as it launched into the air—or rather, attempted to launch. Like a faulty rocket, it arced downward, exploding when it hit the ground. Its smoke was neither pink nor blue. It was black, thick, and pungent as burning oil. Flames leapt in all directions, clinging to guests and trees and cars alike. As the explosion's echo faded, the screams escalated. Burning guests did a stop-drop-and-roll routine while others ripped tablecloths off of still-set tables to smother the flames.

Emily was on fire, two tendrils of sticky, flaming tar burning through her dress. Jacob smacked Emily's belly to put out the flames, momentarily unconcerned with the baby inside her. When the flames were out, Jacob shook his hand, bright red from the heat. Whipping his head around, he spied Garrett howling and rolling on the ground, unquenched flames licking his legs.

"Stay here," Jacob told Emily before running to his friend.

Emily winced and used her elbows to prop herself into a sitting position. She was no longer on fire, but others behind her were, and the tree in front of her most certainly was, flames climbing upward with the swiftness of a frightened squirrel. The burned parts of her belly stung, and she held her breath as she peeled the singed dress away from the wound. The flesh beneath had risen, bubbled, and blackened into two thin, curved points—both somehow identical.

A cackle cascaded through the camp, and this time, everyone snapped to attention. About fifty feet up, there was a black shape hovering between two burning trees. The thing had horns and wings, but the wings weren't flapping. The creature remained suspended in air, its entire body vibrating so intensely that it was hard to make out its dimensions through the blur. Someone behind Emily screamed and fled. Only, the patter of footfalls didn't last long. The creature blinked out of sight in a puff of smoke, and the fleeing person gasped. Emily turned around just in time to see the creature whisking Jacob into the air, blurry talons burning into him, smoke rising from his shoulders. The creature rocketed upward, its laughter and Jacob's scream trailing behind, pitch warping to a lower register. When the thing burst through the canopy, flames sparked the leaves and spread outward in a fast-expanding circle of destruction. Emily gawked, looking for her husband and the creature. Seconds of waiting felt like hours. Someone shook her shoulder, but she paid them no mind.

Then, a fireball barreled toward Earth. It was her husband—minus his skin—limbs flailing and crackling as he plummeted. The impact of wet, crunching bone snapped Emily out of her trance. She screamed and allowed whoever was tugging her shoulder to lead her away. It was her mother. Hanging from the woman's other arm was Emily's limping father. They made their way toward the truck, one labored step at a time. Around them, the forest disintegrated into ash, Jacob's outdoor church crumbling after its thousand years of glory.

"He can't drive," Maureen said, coughing through the smoke. "Give me his keys, Em!"

Emily fished through her wheezing father's pockets, then tossed the keys to her mother. Some guests had already peeled away in their cars, but the rest were still scrambling for an exit. If they weren't careful, they'd all be jammed together on the narrow road, car caskets entombed between burning redwoods. Emily helped her father into the truck's passenger seat, then squeezed herself into the back. Brushing against the door frame, she inhaled sharply and clutched her belly. She barely had the door shut behind her before

Maureen zoomed away, cutting in front of someone else who veered into a tree to avoid colliding with the truck. Emily glanced back, hoping the person—Garrett, it looked like—would still be able to make it out. But there was no time to worry about the others.

Maureen roared down the dirt road with little concern for wildlife-crossing signs. If they hit a deer, they hit a deer. It was better than being trapped by an impassable flaming log.

An hour of white-knuckled driving passed before they made it out of the park, forest giving way to four-lane black-top. Emily could already hear the helicopters traveling toward what was now probably a massive fire.

"You tell no one about this, okay?" Maureen said, and then, remembering Jacob, added, "I'm sorry, Em. I really am. I wish—"

"Stop it, Mom." Emily's tone was flat.

She rested her head on the cool glass of the window, letting the vibrations calm her. Her throat still burned with smoke, but if she breathed slow enough, it offset the pain. She wondered if she was supposed to be crying. That seemed like the appropriate response to all this. Had it not happened yet because she was in shock, or—

There was a kick in her womb, or rather two simultaneous kicks. They felt sharper than normal, and she almost yelped. But when she looked down, the sight stole her breath —two needled points pressing outward, straining the flesh, pushing far harder than Emily figured a baby was capable of.

"Please, please, please stop," Emily whispered, her words thin and breathy.

"What?" her mother asked from the front seat.

The thing inside Emily eased its pressure, the two points receding back into her womb and returning her belly to its smooth, round shape. Emily breathed deep, trying not to sob.

Out of nowhere, the winged creature swooped down to

Emily's window, floating soundlessly and keeping pace with the truck. Had it been following them this whole time, creating a false sense of security before making a grand reentrance? Emily clasped a hand over her mouth, not wanting to frighten her mother while she was driving. The creature was draped in Jacob's loose, singed skin, its trembling wings poking out through two holes in the back. Yellow, catlike eyes gazed at Emily through Jacob's eyelids, which flapped in the wind.

While the creature's mouth didn't move, a voice entered Emily's head—ethereal, but most certainly Jacob's.

You didn't think I'd abandon our child, did you?

SMALLER

D r. Hollis is the first to notice the change in your body. You're a full inch shorter than your last checkup. Strange for a twenty-six-year-old, but not unheard of. You joke that you're not in the NBA anymore, so it shouldn't be a problem. Hollis laughs, and so do you. Yours sounds raspy— aged, like your shrinking frame. Or maybe that's just how it sounds in your head.

Hollis says to mind your blood pressure. Exercise, eat a healthy diet, avoid stress. "Are you stressed? Things all right at work? Home? Anyway, take this pamphlet. Come back in a year, okay?"

When you get home, Oren is sitting at his computer playing *League of Legends*. You kiss him on the cheek, and he pulls his head away. He can't see the screen, damnit. Insults spill from his mouth like a dam breaking—"fucking idiot," "dumbass," and "stupid little bitch." A constant stream. None directed at you, thankfully, but rather some acne-riddled preteen from Milwaukee.

You tell Oren about your doctor visit, all while he attacks the enemy Nexus and shouts commands at his team like a fascist dictator. High blood pressure sounds like something he might have, too, you suggest. At this, he says of course he has high blood pressure—these fucking cretins are to blame.

Match over. They've lost. Oren drops the r-word and you cringe. He's just angry—he doesn't mean it. At least, that's what you've told yourself the last ten or twenty times he's used the word.

You snap out of your rationalizations, and Oren is in matchmaking once more. This cycle will continue all night. You ask if he wants to do something else—maybe go to the bar or watch a movie together. He grunts—a digital caveman. The match starts, and it's like you never even said anything at all. He's back to screaming at the screen, his blood pressure well on its way to becoming a Guinness World Record.

You think back three years to the Grindr profile that first reeled you in—"you better like 'em fiery, 'cause I don't cum any other way." After dating the dullest accountant pillow prince imaginable, fiery was what you wanted and what you got.

Too bad fire burns everything in its path. You wake up each morning denying your burns: the bubbling scar tissue, the acrid fumes of ashen hair. Perhaps it felt nice at first—like a sauna in the middle of winter. Weren't those the days?

You load up a movie you know Oren can't resist—*The Fellowship of the Ring*—and wait for him to notice. Maybe it's enough to pull him away from his computer, to get him to cuddle with you on the couch—how long has it been since you two did that? Oren doesn't budge, even as you watch the opening scene and turn up the volume. The movie is cheesy and hasn't aged well, but if it draws him in, the overextended runtime will have been worth it.

You jump when Oren lets out a "fuck" that's sure to wake the upstairs neighbors. The League of Legends servers are down, apparently, and you try your best to feign sympathy.

You ask if he wants to watch the movie instead, but he's already plugged his headphones into his computer and opened up an internet browser. It's not long before porn pops up on the screen featuring dudes lighter-skinned and more muscular than you'll ever be. You get up from the couch and walk over to Oren, sliding your hand down to his waist. He brushes it away—says he'll be done soon.

In no time, the movie is off, you're out of the apartment, and Oren is cleaning himself up, happy to see the League of Legends servers are working again.

You walk to the bar even though it's barely five o'clock. A drink will calm you down and douse the fire. At least, for now. There are no conscious thoughts as you navigate; you could get to Stubby's blindfolded. Of course, that's nothing to brag about. Perhaps even something you should have mentioned to Dr. Hollis? Maybe at next year's checkup.

Something disrupts your unconscious navigation, and suddenly you're facedown on the sidewalk. You tripped. On what? Your pant leg, it looks like. Got caught under your shoe and sent you tumbling like you were already drunk. It doesn't make much sense, though. You're still wearing a belt, and a tailor had these jeans altered just for you. So how do four inches of fabric catch on your heel? No time to think on it—just roll the legs up into fashionable folds and keep walking. The bar's close by now.

The bartender preps your drink before you even say a word. It makes you hate yourself, so you walk right back out the bar and go. Steve Franklin Wosnick—you know the bartender's full name—calls out to you as you leave; something about your tab. You ignore him and head toward a different bar; one much farther away but hopefully humiliation-free.

Hours later, you stagger home in the dark, stumbling in the path of honking cars and cursing bicyclists. None of them hit you, and you're not sure whether to be grateful or bummed. You trip on your pants again. The legs are still rolled up from earlier, and the belt still grips your waist, but somehow the fabric finds its way under you. You stare at your feet and vomit, acid and vodka soaking into your shoes. *God, what a night. What a fucking night.*

When you get home, Oren's not there. The clock reads 1:33 a.m. Oren works at eight in the morning. *Where the hell could he be?*

But you know already.

You know about the one person on League of Legends Oren doesn't scream at, doesn't call "shit for brains." The one person he whispers to through his headset, glancing around to make sure you aren't listening. But you are listening. You have been for months. Yet he has never said anything explicitly incriminating. You've heard snippets like "I'll come up with something" and "make it out there sometime," though. Apparently "sometime" meant tonight, just six hours before work.

You flop into bed, which feels bigger than usual. Not just because Oren is gone but, well, because of what's been happening today. The doctor's measurements? Tripping on your tailored pants? Yeah, there's something to that. Normally your legs poke off the edge of the bed and you have to fold them in, afraid some monster will nibble at them. (It's childish, but we all have that child in us sometimes, don't we?) But tonight, you fit perfectly in the bed and don't have to fold up like an accordion. In fact, there's an extra foot of stretch space, something you've wanted for years but now couldn't want less. *What is happening here?*

Sobbing wears you out after an hour or two—your tear ducts dry, and your face muscles are sore. Alcohol sloshes through your aching body, burning and sedating in equal measure. Oren doesn't come home. You fall asleep thinking about death. Oren's, your own. Whoever's.

WHEN YOU WAKE UP, the change is undeniable. Your blanket—which normally only covers either your head or your toes but never both at once—now envelops your whole body with extra fabric to spare on all sides. You thrash to get the blanket off, thinking you might still be dreaming, but as soon as you escape, you understand this to be reality. The sun pierces your thin curtains and floods your vision like a hangover death ray. But the pain isn't confined to your head: It's spread to all extremities. You've never had a hangover like this one, not even in the college semester you failed because, as you told your mom, you'd spent too much time with your Buds. Though you didn't tell her it was Buds with a capital B.

You contemplate pulling the blanket back over your head, but by this point you see how much you've shrunk. The size of a Chucky doll, and perhaps just as murderous with your hangover from hell. *No.* You must be asleep. None of this is possible, right? You pinch yourself. Slap yourself. Bite your hand as hard as you can. *Definitely awake.* A crescent of blood blooms on your palm.

You scoot to the edge of the bed, and the drop down seems precipitous. Landing on the ground nearly topples you. You head to the bathroom, noting how long it takes to get there with your shortened strides. The bathroom mirror is up too high to reach, so you climb onto the toilet first, then the sink. From there, you can at least see your face—shrunken, puffy, and ringed around the eyes. The tears come once more, and along with them pain from the alcohol's resistance as your body tries to break it down. Seconds later, your chest is

covered in vomit and you practically pass out, only to stabi-
lize yourself with one tiny hand against the mirror.

You jump into the bath because what else is there to do
but take the longest shower of your life? Maybe you're like
one of those dinosaur toys that grow in water—the old kids'
toy you and your brother got such a kick out of. You'll soak
up the water and return to your normal size, just like that.
Problem solved. The hot water washes away the vomit, and
since you're having trouble standing, you sit instead. The
only way to measure time is by how quickly the water cools.

The water makes its way to the drain, and after a while
your body begins to move with it. Minutes ago, you were
large enough to avoid being carried away, but not anymore.
The drain approaches, and though you're still too big to go
down it, that might not last for long. You scramble to get up,
straining for a handhold to pull you out of the shower, but
it's out of reach. The room is thick with moisture, and it feels
like you're barely getting any air. A panic attack is imminent.

And then you hear it—the clack of a key turning and the
creak of the apartment door. Oren's back, the cheating
bastard. Scratch that—your loving savior is back. You scream
for him, but even then, your voice comes out small, no louder
than the shower itself. If you know anything about his
routine, it's that he'll be at his computer, headphones on,
within minutes. From the kitchen comes the beep and hum
of the microwave. Soon, you smell burning Hot Pocket. Oren
shouts "god damnit," and you shout right back at him from
the shower. It's the shout of a mouse about to be scooped up
by a hawk.

The water feels more like a strong undertow than a
stream now. You have a minute, maybe less, to catch Oren's
attention.

At the back of the shower is Oren's razor, clogged with
pubes. *Of course,* it is. He used to shave for you when you first

started dating, but that was only to make a sexy first impression. Come to think of it, in the past three years, he hasn't shaved once, not since that first date. If he's doing it again, he's definitely cheating. You make your way to the razor, bracing yourself through the current and the water pelting you from above—much more intense now, given your diminutive size. You cling to the razor as if it were a life raft, still screaming for Oren.

You scream for hours—your vocal cords shredded to useless, vibrating meat—but Oren never comes. Eventually, you lose consciousness.

<hr>

WHEN YOU WAKE, the world is moving upward at a gut-wrenching pace. You're still on the razor, and the razor is in Oren's hand, heading toward his face. How small are you now? Small enough to fit between the rubber grooves on the razor's handle. You're an ant, sticking to surfaces without even trying. But you're not immune to motion sickness, and the razor rocks back and forth against Oren's cheek. The sound of shaving from so close is deafening, like sandpaper scraping against gristle. *This is the end, isn't it?* He'll wash off the razor, flush you down the sink, and won't give a second thought to what became of you. For all he knows, you went back to your parents' house in Indiana and decided to stay. Good riddance, he probably thinks. Makes the whole ignore-you-'til-you-break-up-with-me thing a lot easier and less drawn out. Is that what he's been shooting for?

You scream again because as hard and impossible as life might be right now, dying has never been your plan. Not seriously, anyway. Oren holds his razor out to examine it, not because he heard you but because he cut himself. His blood drips from the blade toward the handle, and in seconds, you're awash in it, barely keeping your head above the crimson ocean of the bead.

Oren turns on the sink. *This is it.* He holds the razor out toward the water and then . . . then he stops. He squints, looks closer, sees you. Stares. His face pale, half-shaven, drizzling blood.

After what feels like an hour of staring, he turns off the sink and carries you away on the razor, holding it like an overfull cup of tea, tiptoeing through the living room and into the bedroom. He sets you down on the bed, leaves the room, and comes back a few minutes later with a plate full of toast and a bowl full of water. You're crying the tiniest teardrops now, no bigger than grains of silt.

Oren sits on the edge of the bed, and the shift would feel like an earthquake had he not done it so softly. He looks you in the eyes, holding your gaze for longer than he has in the past couple of years combined.

"Listen," he says, his voice soft. "I didn't mean for this to happen again."

Again?

"Forget about me, okay?" he continues. "The quicker you do, the quicker you'll be, uh . . . you know, back to normal."

He sits in silence for a moment, wringing his hands.

"I'm moving in with Jeremy. And before you say anything —if you even can—yeah, I know. I'm an asshole. But that's good news, too, isn't it? You don't have to live with an asshole anymore."

Oren stands abruptly, and you lose your footing. Some water from the bowl spills out onto the sheets.

"I'm gonna leave now," Oren says. "It might be a few days before you turn back, so that's, uh . . . that's what the water and toast are for. It took a few days the first time this happened, and the guy almost . . . never mind. Anyway, should be enough to, uh, well—"

Oren's cheeks are bright red, and not just from the shaving accident.

"Jesus," he says. "I just wish I knew why this keeps happening."

He grabs the razor off the bed to finish shaving, then heads to the bedroom door. Before leaving, he turns around.

"Hey, when you're full-size again, can you text me? Just give me a heads-up. We can delete each other's numbers after that. I'd just really hate to, uh, not know . . . you know?"

He lingers in the doorway for a moment, glancing away from you, then nods. Minutes later, he's gone. You'll never see him again.

———

DAYS PASS, and you survive on crumbs of toast and droplets of water. There's little else to do but weep and try to forget, like Oren suggested. Your phone rings, but you can't answer it. Probably your job calling to fire you or Mom calling to see why you've been so distant lately.

Your body is still the same when you wake up the second morning, the third, and the fourth. It is so small and so full of pain—so much pain, you fear that it'll kill you.

Cruelly enough, it doesn't.

The fifth morning is different, though. The toast has gone moldy, and the water bowl filmy. But you've changed too. You're bigger. Maybe just by an inch or so, but you're bigger. And the day after that, a few more inches. Then a few more. Sometimes you worry your bones are growing faster than your skin and will pierce the surface, but it never happens. Still, your limbs itch and tingle as if you slept on them weirdly, a feeling that lasts for days.

By the time two weeks have passed, you're almost full-

size. You'll never quite be back to normal, but you're func-
tioning—at least kind of.

When you're big enough to reach the computer, you pull
up Facebook and look up the name you've been obsessed
with the past few days: Ben Matheson, Oren's boyfriend
before you. The message you send is simple:

*Oren just broke up with me. It's hard to explain, but I need to talk
to you.*

Ben's reply is immediate: *I know what you want to talk about.
When can you meet? I'm already in contact with the others. We'll
make sure he can never do this again.*

You meet the next afternoon. You, Ben, and the dozen
others. All of you are shorter than most men, some of you
especially so. And yet, by the time you all part ways—with a
plan set and strategies devised—each of you stands just a
little taller.

Oren has no clue what's coming.

GHOST OF AN OCEAN

"Lonely" and "lovely" are just one letter apart, and the Sandhills exist in their overlap. Here, the land bobs up and down like waves. It undulates on a geologic scale, hills eroding into valleys and valleys growing into hills one drifting grain at a time. This place used to be an ocean, and whenever I drive its winding highway I imagine a mile of water above me. As long as I don't roll down the windows, I'm safe from sharks.

These thoughts keep me pleasantly distracted as I drive to Browning a full month before the university's summer session ends. I'm missing my senior year finals and will probably fail my classes, lose my scholarship, and forfeit any last hope of getting a degree. But what other choice do I have? Mom can no longer hide the swell of her tumor under an oversized sweater, and I can literally hear Dad's tumor when we talk on the phone, that bulge under his tongue turning Rs into Ws. My Bio professor says I should be safe coming home as long as I drink only bottled water and don't eat food made with local ingredients, Mom's green bean casserole included. That's the cruel irony; the pesticide lingers invisibly in what keeps us alive. Now, it's banned the world over, of course, but Browning will feel its effects for generations to come. That is, if there are more generations.

Scratching is my anxious habit of choice, and I claw at the brown splotch on my arm. Every time I examine it, it looks bigger, but I tell myself I'm just imagining things. I inhale deeply and picture myself once more at the bottom of that prehistoric ocean, a hundred million years distant from my troubles. But the scene evaporates when I see a middle-aged man on the side of the road. He stands behind the shimmer of asphalt, translucent heat snaking upward. His back is propped against a fence post, and he's holding out his thumb. Hitchhikers might be the relic of a more reckless and carefree time, but there's no one around for miles. Who else is going to help the guy? I pull over.

The man's face is as bumpy as the surrounding hills, and bright red—sunburn on sunburn on sunburn, stacked all the way to the bone. I wince, but he grins through the pain. Holding up a massive tan duffle bag, he points to the back seat. I nod and unlock the door. His bag lands on the leather with a sound like clinking glass.

"What you got in there?" I ask, and immediately regret my nosiness.

The man climbs into the passenger seat and balls his hands into fists. For a moment I think he'll throw a punch, dump me on the blistering asphalt, and peel away in my car. But instead he unclenches his hand, slow as a blooming flower.

"A miracle," he says. His voice is not what I expect—so deep it sounds underwater.

I smile and resist the urge to laugh as I pull back onto the road. This character will keep me entertained until I get to Browning. For my sake, it'd be convenient if he lived there, but for his sake, I hope he doesn't.

"Where you headed?" I ask.

The man tugs his hand as if pulling on a glove. It looks like there's an extra inch of skin hanging limp at the end of his fingers, no muscle or bone underneath for support. I do a double take, glancing up at the road to make sure I won't crash before returning to the man, but on second look, his hands seem perfectly normal—calloused and lean with dirt-darkened creases. Farmer's hands.

"I'm bound for a town just northwest of here," he says.

"Sounds like we're headed to the same place. I don't think I've seen you in town before. Just visiting?"

Truth be told, unless you live in Browning, the only good reason for stopping there is to fill up your gas tank. But if you read the big Browning news—a national headline for one day before the world stopped caring—I suppose morbid curiosity might draw you to the place.

"No, no," the man says. "I've been here a *long* time."

His low voice rumbles like a whale call, and I swear it rattles the car. The way he speaks seems to stretch out time, each word galaxies from the next. And I can't explain it, but when his mouth finally closes, it feels like years have come and gone. The sky—blue just moments ago—bleeds streaks of pink and orange. While the watercolors of heaven have brought me peace on countless slow summer evenings, seeing them this time turns my stomach.

Nerves bristling, I clear my throat. Maybe I can shake the feeling through small talk, something us Nebraskans are good at.

"So, what's your Browning connection?" I ask.

He gives me a blank stare and says nothing.

"Relatives, friends, childhood home?" I ask, that bristly feeling not going away.

"What's Browning?" he asks.

I try to detect a curling lip or crinkling eye—anything to

indicate he's pulling my leg—and find nothing. But before I can tell him that's the name of the town, he closes his eyes. His eyelids twitch rapidly as if he's fallen into REM sleep. I feel a tug at the back of my neck, like I'm a kitten being yanked by its scruff. A muscle cramp? No, doesn't feel like it. But whatever it is locks my neck in place. The car veers off road and plows through a patch of cacti before I'm able to correct course. The man doesn't notice my off-roading, or if he does, there's no indication that it worries him. All at once, my neck loosens and my head feels lighter both physically and mentally. As I pull back onto the pavement, cactus spines dislodge from my tires and clink against the car's under-carriage.

"Sorry about that," I say, my cheeks flushing. "I—I'm not sure what—"

"Browning," the man says, opening his eyes. "Town in northwest Nebraska. Population 2,054 as of 1970, but likely much lower now."

"Yes, that's . . . I think that's right."

But suddenly, I'm not so sure. The word "Browning" has stopped sounding familiar, and I scavenge my memory for even a hint of its meaning. Somehow, my mind arrives at the family barn in the years before its eventual snowstorm collapse. My dad, shotgun in hand, walks a younger me through the red double doors, leading me to my first lesson on mercy. *Marielle isn't getting any better*, he says. *See that lump under her eye?* The lump makes her look like she's squinting all mean-like. I hide behind Dad's leg. He cocks the gun. *I won't make you do this one, but you'll have to do another someday.* Fifteen years later, I still haven't. But maybe Dad didn't mean putting down cows. My mind returns to Browning. What the hell is Browning?

"When I last visited," the man says, "the town was called something else."

I shiver. A silence descends on the car, and there's only the faint whistle of wind blowing through the door's faulty weather stripping. My throat constricts, and as stupid as it sounds, I feel like it'll close up if I don't keep talking. I realize the man and I haven't been formally introduced, so I stutter my name before asking him his.

"I'm Brandon, by the way. What's your name?"

But before he can speak it, his name pulses up into my consciousness like puss from a wound. I try to picture its spelling, but written language captures only a crude approximation of the sound. One acidic syllable after another bubbles up, long buried and yearning to be heard. The name is endless. As it gets louder, I lose focus on the road and my car swerves between lanes. Realizing I haven't been breathing, I gasp for air and slam on the brakes. My car fishtails to a halt. On a busier highway I might've collided with someone in the opposite lane, but out here, I'm completely alone: just me and the man. Car in park, I roll down the window and smash my palms against my ears. I refuse to hear more of his name; it will destroy me. And I know that sounds foolish, but my gut instinct is strong. I'm prepared to run, to abandon my vehicle and take my chances out in that sprawling ghost of an ocean, never mind the coyote packs howling back and forth from one side of the highway to the other.

The creature shifts to face me in his seat. His eyes briefly retract into his skull, then squelch back into place against his eyelids—a zoom lens set in flesh. I'm paralyzed.

"Your people used to love me," he says.

I say nothing, unable to fathom how anyone could love this creature. It continues speaking, each word the distance between a star's first spark and last sputter.

"But they tossed me aside when life was good, assuming it would stay that way without my intervention. They were wrong. I see it in this man's pestilence."

The creature rips the filthy sleeve off its button-up shirt, but human skin pulls away with it. Tiny black scales gleam underneath, and each one rises from the flesh as if inhaling. Before I can get a better look, the creature tugs its disguise back into place. It's then that I notice the human skin's raised brown splotches. They mirror the ones on my body but are much larger. Perhaps mine will grow to that size, too, a possibility I've been ignoring by burying my head in school work.

"He would have died within weeks," the creature says. "An entirely preventable death, but this land punishes those who have little to spare. Now, because of his willing sacrifice, I have a face that humans will not run from, though I admit this skin is an imperfect fit."

I picture the farmer's peeled corpse dumped in the hills, sunbaked and beaded black with flies. Coyotes will find him before people do, and then he'll be nothing more than bones.

"Please, don't kill me," I say. "I'll do anything. You can have my car. Just—"

The creature reaches into the back seat, careful not to let its human skin slough off again. And this is it. This is the end. I'm sure of it. Somehow, I know running won't save me; my legs aren't fast enough. That thing will pull a gun from the bag, or perhaps an alien weapon, something humans haven't yet dreamed up despite our boundlessly cruel imagination. All I ask for is a quick death.

But what the creature pulls out is not a weapon. It's a translucent pink crystal the size of a thimble. Its center is hollow, containing a few drops of liquid.

"Your people will love me," the creature says. "And I will end their plague."

Death seems less certain than it did moments ago, but I remain statue-still, halfway out of the car, trembling hands gripping the door. The receding sunlight glints off the bag's remaining contents—thousands more of the crystals.

"With this," the creature says, snapping the crystal open and pouring its contents over the farmer's cancerous skin. "I will save them from sickness."

The liquid sizzles and foams against the raised brown patch. I've seen plenty of similar chemical reactions in science labs, but this is the first to make me gag. I picture the mystery liquid burning its way through the skin to those fish-like scales underneath. But when I look up from the ground, there's a smell like honeysuckle. The fizzing recedes into silence like an antacid tablet dissolved in water, and when the creature wipes away the foam, the cancerous splotch is gone. I'm gaping. The creature takes out a second crystal.

"I sense you, too, are afflicted," it says, offering the crystal to me. "All I ask for in exchange is love."

The creature leans in and stares at me, unblinking. Up close, its eyes appear inhuman—pupils too large, whites too small. And perhaps it's warping my mind again, but I sense compassion in the creature's gaze. That, and eons of loneliness. I don't think I'm imagining it.

The sun is almost gone now, its light fuzzy on the rim of the hills. Long, curving shadows spread across the highway. It will be dark soon, and my parents will be expecting me.

I remember Mom falling when we spoke on the phone last week. She claimed she tripped on an upturned corner of the rug, but I didn't hear her walking around before that. I think her body just gave out. Dad wheezed as he tried to help her up, a process that took minutes when it should have taken seconds. When I asked if they were okay, they assured me everything was fine, failing to hide their gasps for air. I hung up the phone and tried not to cry.

"Will you take me to your people?" the creature asks.

It's June, but night is coming on and there's a chill in the air. The highway's shimmering heat has vanished. Overhead, the black silhouette of a nighthawk cries out—one sharp note signaling that the stars aren't far behind.

I nod at the creature, climb back into the car, and start the engine. We drive home, soon to be born again.

WHEN MOTHMAN CAME TO
QUEER LAKE

Ellie and I fled Crawford after our big secret came out—pun intended. The mom-and-pop grocery store owner Mr. Reynolds caught us kissing behind the Dumpster and fired us on the spot. We were off the clock and out of uniform, but the man couldn't have homos scaring customers into shopping at Wal-Mart.

He was shocked when we filed a wrongful termination lawsuit, and he nearly fainted when we won in court. Our winnings were enough to score us a plot of land far away from Crawford, complete with a fishing pond and golden prairie as far as the eye could see. Thus, the town of Queer Lake was born. The fact that the state didn't officially recognize it as a town only made Queer Lake queerer.

Ellie built us a house with slanted floors and enough cracks for mice to nestle in (as if I could do any better), but there was still the problem of food. It was a two-hour drive to the nearest grocery store—yep, *that* grocery store—which gave us all the push we needed to grow our own crops. Learning to farm was a joyful process, though. We would till rows in the soil and make *corny* jokes about what we were planting. When the exhaustion set in, we'd spend the evenings cuddling and watching *X-Files* on our shitty antenna TV. On the rare occasion that we got tired of spending every second together, it was easy to give each other space: Ellie fished the pond while I wandered the hills and tried to avoid prairie dog holes. But on those hikes, I often found myself glancing back at Ellie, admiring her arm muscles as she reeled in catfish, the rod bending under their weight. I could never stay away for long.

However, paradise came with the anxiety that it might crumble at any second. We'd seen energy company vans stopping on the road in front of our house. The workers surveyed the land, taking notes and measurements of who-knows-what. Ellie thought they might be planning the route of an oil pipeline—a black snake that would soon plunge its fangs into Queer Lake.

A more familiar threat also drove that road: trucks sporting Confederate flags and bumper stickers for homophobic senators. Whenever those drove by, Ellie and I went inside, not wanting the drivers to see us holding hands. You'd think we'd be safe doing that out in the middle of nowhere, but apparently not.

Then came Mothman, our strangest visitor by far. We'd first learned about him as children from a library book about cryptids. But it wasn't until two decades later, as we returned from the fields, that we saw him for ourselves, perched atop our house. Ellie dropped her armful of corn, and I about pissed myself. Mothman was a tall, dark silhouette in the twilight. His eyes were large and red as stoplights, and his wings were long enough to graze the gutters on both sides of the roof. Spotted, he flew upward falcon-fast and disappeared into the clouds. We craned our necks for a good while, waiting for him to reappear, but by the time the clouds passed, the horizon had already swallowed the sun. As we made our way inside, I glimpsed a quick, black shape passing over the moon, but by then I was disinclined to trust my eyes.

We sat on the couch in the dark for a while before either of us could speak. Unsure what else to say, I broke the silence.

"Want to watch *X-Files?*"

"Pretty sure we just did," Ellie replied.

I snorted, trying to hold back a laugh, but the dam burst. Both of us fell into a fit of giggles. Tearing up and gasping for breath, Ellie collapsed into my lap.

A *thunk* on the roof halted our laughter. We stared at each other through the darkness, and neither of us dared breathe.

A minute of silence, then Ellie whispered, "It's him, right?"

"It's got to be. Why the hell is he here?"

We'd both seen him, so we weren't crazy. But just because our minds were fine didn't mean everything else was. Where Mothman showed up, tragedy struck. In 1967, he tried to warn the people of Point Pleasant about the impending Silver Bridge collapse, but his omens were esoteric at best, trans-mitted through dreams that left more people scratching their heads than taking action. Forty-six people died in the Ohio River that December, and Mothman vanished.

———

EACH MORNING, Ellie wrote a new tragic prediction on our refrigerator whiteboard: "Ellie will come out as straight," "Wachiwi will develop a corn allergy," or "the mice will eat us in our sleep." Seeing these jokes made me smile, but I couldn't always bring myself to laugh. Had the people of Point Pleasant done the same thing as us, dismissing Mothman's omens only to pay the ultimate price? I mentioned this to Ellie one day as we were harvesting potatoes.

"What if it's something serious?" I said. "A drought. A wildfire. Violent homophobes. Or Proud Boys coming to—you know. I mean, there's nowhere to run out here. No way to protect—"

"Let's not psych ourselves out," she said, wiping her muddy hands on her jeans. "Maybe Mothman was just passing through on his way to Crawford. Plenty of tragedy to warn people about in that shithole. And in any case, don't you trust me to protect you?"

She flashed a flirty smile and flexed her muscular arms. The tension in my chest eased up, and I couldn't help smiling back. I felt silly for worrying in the first place. It had been three weeks since the Mothman sighting, and he hadn't appeared again. It was probably just a fluke.

But Mothman returned that evening. He stood beside the pond, his red eyes reflecting off the water. Ellie and I watched him from the relative safety of our home, daring only to peek through a crack in the curtains. Mothman was shivering. His whole body trembled, and his knees looked close to collaps-ing. When at last he fell, he landed facedown in the pond, his wings twitching in sharp, spastic motions. Ellie and I looked at each other, wide-eyed and frozen. She sprang into action first, running out the door. I hesitated to follow, suspecting a trap, but if Ellie was going to die, I'd die beside her.

We rushed toward the pond, and the closer we got the more I wanted to turn back. Mothman had the wingspan of a pterodactyl and the build of an NBA player; he could easily fuck us up if he wanted to. But that didn't seem to register for Ellie as she barreled forward. She wouldn't be able to pull Mothman out of the water on her own, so I kept following despite every hair on my body bristling.

When we reached Mothman, no bubbles came up from

where his face rested in the pond. I worried we were too late, but we each grabbed a leg and pulled him out. His fuzzy form prickled me with static electricity, only the static didn't discharge after one touch. The sensation was constant as we dragged him onto dry land and, with tremendous effort, tipped him onto his back. Seeing him up close, I could only discern his eyes. Shadows bunched up around his other features as if they weren't for us mortals to see. It was the kind of darkness one might find at the bottom of a well—an amorphous black that banished all light. And while it sounds like I should've been frightened, my heartbeat slowed in his presence.

"His eyes," Ellie said, her voice far away.

I kneeled down to get a better look. Mothman's eyes still glowed with life, and something danced below their glassy surface. It was a swirling mist that vacillated between form and formlessness. I caught glimpses of fire devouring homes, tactical boots crushing necks, and people dying in the streets of some town—distant or near, I couldn't be sure. The images flashed by so quickly that it was hard for me to keep up. But even if I didn't consciously register each one, my unconscious mind still pieced together their meaning. Tears welled in my eyes. Acid rose in my throat. I turned away from Mothman and vomited into the grass.

After my gut emptied and I'd dry heaved several times, I turned back to Ellie. She was no longer looking at Mothman. Instead she stared off into space, her knees pulled to her chin. My gaze lowered to Mothman, and I realized he was still breathing—hyperventilating, really, the rise and fall of his chest quick and shallow. Not knowing what else to do, I placed a hand on him and moved it in soft, slow circles. The static sensation prickled me even more than before, but the longer I spent soothing him, the weaker the sensation became. Eventually it diminished to nothing more than gentle moth fuzz against my skin.

Mothman's wing twitched away a horsefly—one of the last still alive before the frost. I stepped back. After a minute of strained movement, Mothman pushed himself onto his feet. He looked at Ellie, then at me. At least for now, his eyes didn't swirl with a thousand omens. I held his gaze for what felt like hours, wondering if it held a message. With little warning, he took off into the night to carry on his work.

When the black sky consumed him, Ellie shuffled over and hugged me from behind. She sniffled, and her cheek felt wet against my neck.

"I think this place is his sanctuary too," Ellie said, her voice hoarse.

A truck roared down the road. While I could only see the headlights, I pictured a driver with a MAGA hat inside. I pictured him getting out of the truck with a rifle in hand. I pictured hate pouring from his mouth and screams pouring from Ellie's. I pictured two unmarked graves. An energy company laying down pipe. Our home demolished. Our pond shimmering with the wrong kind of rainbow, black and viscous.

That night, I dreamed about Crawford and the world we left behind. Ellie woke me when I started screaming in my sleep. And as grateful as I was to wake up in Queer Lake, I could feel that other world encroaching on our paradise. It was not a matter of *if* it would reach us but *when*. I wondered where Mothman would rest after this place was swallowed up.

ACKNOWLEDGMENTS

First and foremost, I want to thank my partner, Kate. In addition to being hilarious, intelligent, and compassionate, she has always supported my creative work, even when our tastes differed. I love her deeply and I am grateful that the years have only brought us closer.

I also want to thank my beta readers. Without them, this book never would have happened. Thanks to Dizzy Gabrielle, a lifelong friend and phenomenal critique partner. Thanks to my lovely writing group: Marc Woodman, Ashley Novak, Aryn Huck, Grace Stallworth, and Meghan Leadabrand; I always enjoy our workshops. Thanks to Anthony Engebretson, an excellent workshopper and comrade. Thanks to Eric LaRocca, whose critiques and publishing advice have helped immensely. Thanks to Sam Richard, a great friend, supporter, and inspiration. Thanks to Gabino Iglesias, Patrick Barb, Patrick Tumblety, Lilyn George, Donyae Coles, Cynthia Gómez, Danny Marks, Gordon B. White, Oscar Lee Krinket, and William Sterling. All of them helped make this book a reality.

Thanks to Rae Oestreich for the detailed and immensely helpful edits.

Thanks to Matthew Revert for the killer cover design.

Thanks to my writing teachers over the years, especially Deborah McGinn, who sparked my love of writing.

Thanks to my parents and my sister. I appreciate how supportive they've been of all my obnoxious, concerning interests. Much love!

And last, shout-out to all the weird, queer anti-capitalists out there. This book is for you.

STORY NOTES

MOTHER'S TONGUE

I got the idea for this story after watching *Free Solo*, a documentary about rock climber Alex Honnold, who decided to climb El Capitan with no gear whatsoever. What disturbed and fascinated me most about this film was his complete disregard for both the deadly risk involved and his partner's reasonable fears on the matter. Basically, "Mother's Tongue" is *Free Solo* turned Weird.

IVORY (ORIGINALLY PUBLISHED IN *FEVER DREAM*)

I've been fascinated with both birds and cryptids my entire life. And what's a more cryptid-like bird than the ivory-billed woodpecker? It's been extinct for a while now, but every few years there's a new possible sighting reported. I wanted to write a story about this extinct bird coming back into existence to carry out some bizarre, unknowable mission. Thus, "Ivory" was born.

GRAY MATTER

Dementia terrifies me. My grandparents have suffered from it, and while I hope to never experience it myself, the possibility is always there. Exploring this disease as a monster in "Gray Matter" helped me cope with that fear somewhat. Fear aside, I had a blast writing this story, though I will probably never look at liquid plumber the same way again.

SICK LEAVE

I'm lucky to have a job with paid sick leave, but many workers don't. It's a sad fact of life under capitalism that people are forced to work while deathly ill. The alternative, staying home, often means losing money or even losing a job. Of course, working while sick leads to problems of its own. "Sick Leave" deals with this issue through the lens of the Weird.

THE PATCH

The Great Pacific Garbage Patch has horrified me ever since I first learned of its existence. I'd tell you how big it is, but by the time this book comes out, its size will have changed—hopefully shrunk, if we're lucky. In any case, it's a big garbage soup in the middle of the ocean. In "The Patch," I imagined this soup becoming so massive that it gained godlike powers and, like a god, demanded worship. It's a slightly goofy premise, but the story was lots of fun to write.

THE LORD ABOVE

Once, when dropping off a rent check at my landlady's crumbling mansion, I discovered a nest of snakes living on her front steps. That story is true. "The Lord Above" is not, but you will probably find truth in its exploration of the land-lord–tenant relationship. Landlords might not be literal vampires, but they are certainly metaphorical ones. With that in mind, I encourage you to send this story anonymously to your landlord. I know vampires can't see themselves in the mirror, but maybe your landlord will see themself in "The Lord Above."

UNDER THE HOOF, UPON THE HORNS

The Running of the Bulls has always struck me as a nasty tradition—men proving their masculinity by putting them-selves in danger, topped off with a spectacle of slaughter. I wanted to explore both toxic masculinity and animal cruelty in "Under the Hoof, Upon the Horns" without being too preachy about either. First and foremost, my goal was to tell a story that felt like a fever dream. This story ended up being one of my favorites in the collection.

FOR MY FINAL GIRL

I'm not a big fan of serial killer stories. Generally, they're too focused on the killer for my taste, and the victim's perspec-tive is much more interesting. That's the idea behind "For My Final Girl." With the exception of a couple scenes, the killer is absent. The central focus is Serena's experience living in fear of the man. My intention was to strike a good balance between empathy and spine-tingling creepiness.

LOCKDOWN

I'm a teacher, so a school shooting is just about the worst nightmare I can imagine. "Lockdown" was tough to write for that reason. I wanted to handle the subject matter sensitively while also injecting it with supernatural horror. Hopefully, there will come a day when this story is no longer relevant.

TOP 5 GHOSTS CAUGHT ON CAMERA

The origins for this story are goofy, but I got the idea from *Nuke's Top 5*, a YouTube channel that mostly features ghost video compilations. Nuke starts many of his videos with the phrase "Top 5 Ghosts Caught on Camera," which became the title for this story. Being a terrible pantser, I had no story outline beyond the fact that there would indeed be five ghosts. I knew the story would be a little tongue-in-cheek, but I also wanted it to circle around some central darkness—a tragedy that would make the story's five parts cohere.

REMI ROOK THE CANNIBAL COOK

I sometimes wish I'd been around at the height of public access television. Of course, I can look up clips of public access shows on YouTube, but it would've been fascinating to see those shows live on an old TV. There was some truly weird stuff that aired. I kept that weirdness in mind when I was writing "Remi Rook the Cannibal Cook." Funny enough, the idea came to me while proctoring the ACT for high school students. Besides observing to make sure they weren't cheating, I had little else to occupy my mind. What strange ideas the brain comes up with in times of great boredom!

MY BETTER HALF (ORIGINALLY PUBLISHED IN *SIRENS CALL*)

I'm bisexual and have sometimes joked about having a "gay half" and a "straight half." Of course, the concept of halves with different orientations has no basis in reality, but some people seem to believe it does. I put that idea to the test in "My Better Half," and the body horror that came from it was the most fun I've had writing in a long time.

THE REVEAL

I wrote this story based on a real-life event in which an explosive gender reveal device started a devastating wildfire. This news story was wild on its own, but I wanted to add a supernatural element—an homage to the demonic pregnancy subgenre. I didn't want to be tactless, though. After all, the real-life wildfire was horribly destructive. With that in mind, I chose to make "The Reveal" less about the wildfire and more about the expecting couple's toxic relationship.

SMALLER (ORIGINALLY PUBLISHED IN *NOVEL NOCTULE*)

The sci-fi classic *The Incredible Shrinking Man* partly inspired "Smaller." I wanted to use the shrinking body as a way to explore negligence in romantic relationships—feeling small when others treat you as if you don't exist. Thankfully, I've never been in a relationship like that, but writing this story helped me imagine what it might be like.

GHOST OF AN OCEAN

A couple years back, I was driving with my partner through the Nebraska Sandhills. It's a gorgeous, dramatic landscape almost entirely devoid of human life, but on the loneliest stretch of highway, we saw a hitchhiker by the side of the road. We didn't pick him up because we were afraid, but my excuse was that "we don't have enough room in the back with the luggage." Still, we wondered what might have happened if we had picked him up. "Ghost of an Ocean" answers that question in a wild way. It's also my "what if Rachel Carson wrote cosmic horror?" story.

WHEN MOTHMAN CAME TO QUEER LAKE

Mothman is my favorite cryptid, and this story gave me a chance to expand his lore in a new direction. I imagined that, given his ability to predict future tragedy and people's tendency to ignore his omens, Mothman must feel traumatized and powerless. We see this side of him come out in "When Mothman Came to Queer Lake." We also see the impossible dream of a life insulated from the rest of the world's pain. Sure, safety, love, and joy are possible, but you can never fully disconnect from hell on Earth. You're plugged in, whether you like it or not.

Mother's Tongue: non-explicit reference to suicide
Ivory: parent death
Gray Matter: dementia, self-harm
Sick Leave: brief instance of racism
The Lord Above: animal death
Under the Hoof, Upon the Horns: child death
For My Final Girl: child death
Lockdown: child death, school shooting
Top 5 Ghosts Caught on Camera: child death, drug overdose
My Better Half: biphobia
The Reveal: brief reference to infertility
Smaller: emotionally abusive relationship, alcoholism
When Mothman Came to Queer Lake: homophobia

ABOUT THE AUTHOR

Eric Raglin (he/him) is a speculative fiction writer, podcaster, and horror literature teacher from Nebraska. He frequently writes about queer issues, the terrors of capitalism, and body horror. His work has been published in *Novel Noctule*, *Dread Stone Press*, and *Shiver*. He was a co-editor for the anthology *ProleSCARYet: Tales of Horror and Class Warfare*. He also hosts the Cursed Morsels podcast. Find him at ericraglin.com or on Twitter @ericraglin1992.